RED SOX Drawing Board

25 Years of Cartoons by Eddie Germano

The Stephen Greene Press
Pelham Books

THE STEPHEN GREENE PRESS/PELHAM BOOKS

Published by the Penguin Group
Viking Penguin Inc., 40 West 23rd Street, New York, New York 10010, U.S.A.
Penguin Books Ltd, 27 Wrights Lane, London W8 5TZ, England
Penguin Books Australia Ltd, Ringwood, Victoria, Australia
Penguin Books Canada Ltd, 2801 John Street, Markham, Ontario, Canada L3R 1B4
Penguin Books (N.Z.) Ltd, 182–190 Wairau Road, Auckland 10, New Zealand

Penguin Books Ltd, Registered Offices: Harmondsworth, Middlesex, England

First published in 1989 by The Stephen Greene Press
Published simultaneously in Canada
Distributed by Viking Penguin Inc.

10 9 8 7 6 5 4 3 2 1

Copyright © Eddie Germano, 1989
Introduction copyright © James Gorman, 1989
All rights reserved.
Mr. Germano's cartoons are reproduced with permission of *The Enterprise*.

Library of Congress Cataloging-in-Publication Data

Germano, Eddie.
Red Sox drawing board : 25 years of cartoons / by Eddie Germano.
p. cm.
ISBN 0-8289-0715-3
1. Boston Red Sox (Baseball team)—Caricatures and cartoons-
-History. I. Title.
GV875.B62G47 1989
796.357'64'09744—dc19 88-24400 CIP

Printed in the United States of America
Set in Melliza by AccuComp Typographers.
Designed by Joyce Weston.
Produced by Unicorn Production Services, Inc.

Except in the United States of America, this book is sold subject to the condition that it shall not, by way of trade or otherwise, be lent, re-sold, hired out, or otherwise circulated without the publisher's prior consent in any form of binding or cover other than that in which it is published and without a similar condition including this condition being imposed on the subsequent purchaser.

Contents

ACKNOWLEDGMENTS...
LOU GORMAN... RED SOX GM... MY SPECIAL THANKS FOR THE BOOK'S INTRODUCTION
OWNER HAYWOOD SULLIVAN WHO OFFERED FULLEST COOPERATION
MARY JANE RYAN... DIR. OF CREDENTIALS WHO ALWAYS MAKES ME FEEL AT HOME
HELEN ROBINSON... WHO GETS MY CALLS THROUGH
TOMMY McCARTHY AND WALTER UNDERHILL... SORELY MISSED
ARTHUR MORRIS... MAKES THE PRESS ROOM FUN
TREASURER JOHN REILLY
THANKS TO DICK BRESCIANI, JOSH SPOFFORD and ALL THE PR STAFF
JACK ROGERS TRAVEL V.P. WHO HANDLES MY SPRING TRAINING SOJOURNS
SUPER GROUNDS MAINTENANCE JOE MOONEY
V.P. OF PROPERTY MANAGEMENT JOE McDERMOTT
DON FITZPATRICK VISITING CLUBHOUSE MGR
SPECIAL THANKS TO COLLEAGUE PETE FARLEY FOR ALL HIS HELP
ARTHUR MOSCATO, RETIRED TICKET DIR.
THANKS TO RETIRED PR DIRECTOR BILL CROWLEY FOR HIS ASSISTANCE
EQUIPMENT MANAGER VINCE ORLANDO
FRANK MacKAY and JIM GATELY
ALWAYS AT YOUR SERVICE IN THE PRESS BOX

JEAN R. YAWKEY... MAJORITY OWNER AND CHAIRWOMAN OF THE BOARD... BOSTON RED SOX
PRESIDENT JOHN HARRINGTON
OVER THE YEARS WITH...
REPORTS
SCOUT SAM MELE
JOHNNY PESKY.. 'MR. RED SOX'
EDDIE KENNEY... PLAYER DEVELOPMENT V.P.
S.I. WRITER PETER GAMMONS
THANKS TO THE LATE FRED MURRAY... MY HIGH SCHOOL BASEBALL COACH
RED SOX PLAYERS COACHES & MANAGERS... THANKS FOR YOUR COOPERATION OVER THE YEARS
REPORTS
SCOUT FRANK MALZONE
MYRON FULLER... PUBLISHER OF THE ENTERPRISE AND BRUCE SMITH... EXECUTIVE EDITOR GIVING ME THE GREEN LIGHT FOR THE BOOK
INSTRUCTOR TED WILLIAMS
DICK O'CONNELL and BUDDY LEROUX FORMER RED SOX EXECUTIVES
AL FORESTER
SOX COUNSEL JOHN DONOVAN...
MY WIFE MARIANNE... AND CHILDREN ANN MARIE... EDWARD AND MICHAEL FOR PUTTING UP WITH MY CRAZY SCHEDULE
NED MARTIN
JOE CASTIGLIONE,
KEN COLEMAN
BOB MONTGOMERY
CURT GOWDY
LONG-TIME FRIENDS FROM RADIO and TV

Introduction

Eddie Germano is one of the few remaining gifted sports cartoonists in America. There was a time in the history of American sports reporting and in-depth sports coverage when numerous sports cartoonists would ply their specialized and skillful trade in sports pages throughout the land. With their brushes and pens they would vividly capture the essence of a sporting event, with all the frustration and agony of a defeat or the ecstatic joy of a victory.

In those years gone by, when almost every sports page had a contributing sports cartoonist, two of my all-time favorites were Willard Mullin, out of New York (and nationally syndicated), and Frank Lanning of the Providence (R.I.) *Journal/Bulletin*. They were so skillful and creative in portraying any sporting event that many readers would search for their sports cartoons first before they would read the sports page itself. Their work, in some instances, became collector's items and more often than not their particular portrayal of an event would be framed and hung on the wall of many a home, tavern, barber shop or office throughout their circulation area. Many of their works would become sports "classics" that were retained by sports fans for decades to come.

The sports writer has the great advantage of having available to him many descriptive words and sentences and paragraphs to relate in detail the ebb and flow of the game; yet the sports cartoonist has but a single image to capture the entire essence of the sporting event.

Eddie Germano is a part of this tradition. He has won his way into the hearts and minds of sports fans throughout all of New England. On many occasions, his works have also become collector's items to be cherished by many a loyal Red Sox fan.

His knowledge and insight into the Red Sox, a team he has loved and followed devotedly for years, is extraordinary. He has spent many a ball game and many a season at Fenway Park, and his friends throughout the sports media of New England and the management personnel of the Red Sox organization are numerous.

His special insights into Red Sox baseball are certain to make this special edition of the Red Sox sports cartoons a beloved treasury for Red Sox fans—not only throughout New England, but throughout the world.

If you are a Red Sox fan you will truly delight in and be entertained by this marvelous collection of Eddie's sports cartoons. They will bring back a flood of Red Sox memories from years gone by.

It may well be that this special collection of Red Sox cartoons by Eddie may become a collector's item that will be highly sought after in the years ahead.

James ''Lou'' Gorman
Senior Vice President/General Manager
Boston Red Sox

1964-1966

These were the wilderness years, when the Red Sox wandered through one bad season after another. Management and players searched in vain for something to pull themselves out of the cellar, while fans sought comfort in a few bright stats: Yastrzemski's slugging, Tony C's home runs. Still, the Sox finished eighth, ninth, and ninth in the league. It was a time to try any fan's loyalty.

TODAY'S OPENER
IN WASHINGTON
PLAY
BALL!
64
RED SOX OPENER
TOMORROW IN N.Y.
EDDIE GERMANO
BROCKTON ENTERPRISE
4/13/64

ONE OF THE ENCOURAGING THINGS ABOUT RED SOX SPRING TRAINING... HAS BEEN THE SHOWING OF FOXBORO'S ELONGATED
GENE CONLEY!
A SORE ARM MADE THE BIG GUY NEXT TO USELESS LAST YEAR AND TO OUR THINKING, THIS WAS A MAJOR REASON FOR THE BOSOX POOR SHOWING
BOSTON
THE BOYS IN SCOTTSDALE SAY GENE'S THROWING ASPIRINS AGAIN.
KEEP IT UP GINO!
IT MUST BE MAKING SMILES COME TO THE COUNTENANCE OF JOHNNY PESKY
EDDIE GERMANO
BROCKTON ENTERPRISE, MASS.
3/18/64
IT APPEARS THE RED SOX HAVE MORE QUESTION MARKS THAN A SENATE INVESTIGATION AS THE START OF THE SEASON DRAWS NEAR...
SOUTHPAW PITCHING
OUTFIELD
CATCHING
3RD BASE
1ST BASE
...BUT YOU CAN PUT AN EXCLAMATION POINT, AFTER THE NAME... BILL MONBOUQUETTE!
THE "GIBRALTAR" OF THE BOSOX PITCHING STAFF
BILL WON TWENTY LAST YEAR WITH A 7TH PLACE CLUB, N' HAS LOOKED GOOD AGAIN THIS SPRING
...AND HE'S GOOD INSURANCE AGAINST ANY PROLONGED LOSING STREAKS!
EDDIE GERMANO
BROCKTON ENTERPRISE
2/3/64

1965

FELIX WAS TOLD TO SCAT WHILE OVER IN THE N.L., AND NOW HE'S THE ALL-STAR STARTING SECOND SACKER FOR THE JUNIOR CIRCUIT NEXT TUESDAY...
...OVER IN THE A.L. FELIX HAS FOUND A HOME AND HAS PROVEN A NICE PET TO HAVE AROUND THE RED SOX HOUSEHOLD
DEFENSIVELY, HE'S NO STAR... BUT GETS THE JOB DONE... WHILE AT BAT, THE FIGURES SPEAK WELL FOR HIM
B
FELIX "THE CAT" MANTILLA
ALL-STAR BERTH
EDDIE GERMANO
BROCKTON ENTERPRISE
7/9/65

1966

IT'S GOOD TO HEAR, SAL "THE BARBER" MAGLIE... IS BACK AS THE RED SOX PITCHING COACH
IF NOTHIN' ELSE, YOU'LL BE IN TRIM THIS SEASON!
THE YOUNG SHAVERS ON THE MOUND STAFF AS WELL AS THE GREYBEARDS, CAN USE A FEW POINTERS FROM THE CAPABLE "OL' LATHER-MASTER"
GEE MR. MAGLIE YOUR JUST IN THE NICK OF TIME
EDDIE GERMANO BROCKTON ENTERPRISE 1/4/66
TED
HALL OF FAME
WHAM
AS HE WAS ACCUSTOMED TO DOING AT THE PLATE, TED WILLIAMS... BROKE DOWN THE DOOR TO THE HALLOWED HALL OF BASEBALL'S ELITE, WITH ONE SWING OF HIS MIGHTY BAT IN THE FIRST YEAR OF ELIGIBILITY WITH A WHOPPING VOTE OF 93.3 %
COME IN, DOGGONE IT! COME IN
GOT A MINUTE MR. VP?
LIST OF PROSPECTS
...AND THE DOOR HAS ALSO BEEN OPENED FOR TED TO TAKE A MORE ACTIVE PART IN ALL RED SOX OPERATIONS
EDDIE GERMANO BROCKTON ENTERPRISE 1/21/66

WITH SO MANY KIDS ON THE ROSTER, 'TIS HOPED OUR RED SOX WILL DIGRESS FROM THE SAME OL' BEAT THIS SEASON...
HOW MONOTONOUS !!!
RED SOX
BANG
LOSE
BANG
WINNING TUNE
HOW SOOTHIN'
SENTIMENTAL OVER YOU
...INSTEAD, 'TIS HOPED THEY'LL PLAY IT SWEET AND MELLOW GLIDING ALONG THE VICTORY ROAD..OUR MUSIC-MAKERS ARE PLAYING THEIR FIRST ROAD DATE OF THE YOUNG CAMPAIGN IN CLEVELAND THIS WEEKEND!
EDDIE GERMANO

LAST WEEKEND WHEN THE INDIANS AND RED SOX MET IN CLEVELAND THEIR PERFORMANCES WERE PURELY OF THE THREE RING VARIETY
WHAT'S SO FUNNY ?
BE A CLOWN BE A CLOWN...
THE WHOLE WORLD LOVES A CLOWN
ME DARE YA!
I DARE YA!
SEE YA THERE!
THE TWO OF 'EM GO AT IT AGAIN TOMORROW AND SUNDAY AT FRIENDLY FENWAY... AND WITH CLEVELAND LEADING THE LEAGUE AND BOSTON FRESH FROM TAKING THE TIGERS (2 of 3) THINGS'LL BE DIFFERENT
EDDIE GERMANO

...NOW A NEW SPEED MERCHANT HAS HIT THE HUB BASEBALL SCENE IN THE PERSON OF THE FLASHIE JOSE TARTABULL, SINCE THE K.C. TRADE, HE'S ALREADY PAID DIVIDENDS TO THE RED HOT REDSOX WHILE STRIKING THE FANCY OF THE FANS
GO
GO
GO
JOSE TARTABULL
AND WHEN WAS THE LAST TIME YOU HEARD THIS KIND OF REACTION AT FENWAY TO A SOX PLAYER?
EDDIE GERMANO

WE DIAMOND CODGERS REMEMBER THE BASE-PATH EXPLOITS OF OL' SAM JETHROE BACK SOME 15 YEARS AGO WITH THE OL' BOSTON BRAVES...
GO
GO
GO
IF SAM COULD SURVIVE GETTING HIT ON THE HEAD WITH AN OUTFIELD FLY, HE WAS WORTH THE ADMISSION PRICE WITH HIS SPEED, AS THE FANS SHOUTED THEIR BOISTEROUS COMMANDS...
SAM JETHROE

1967

It was the year of the Impossible Dream: The Red Sox, 100-to-1 longshots in spring training, clinched the pennant on the last day of the season. Under manager Dick Williams's stern hand, the skills of individual players blended into real teamwork. Yet victory in the World Series, which had eluded Boston since 1918, was again not to be.

THIS YEAR I'M AFRAID OF NOBODY!
A.L. ST.
RED SOX
AFTER A SUCCESSFUL SPRING TRAINING SEASON, THE KID FROM FENWAY WAS READY TO TAKE ON ANYONE ON THE BLOCK...

I MAY LOSE BUT THEY'LL KNOW THEY'VE BEEN IN A FIGHT!
HE CAME OUT OF HIS FIRST SPARRING SESSION WITH CONFIDENCE AND AN EVEN SPLIT VS. CHICAGO...

SOCK
POW
...AND THEN DOWN IN NEW YORK THE KID REALLY GOT TANGLED UP IN A BRAWL AND WITH A LITTLE LUCK HE MIGHT HAVE WON ALL THREE OF HIS BOUTS INSTEAD OF JUST ONE...BUT ONE THING WAS PROVEN, THIS YEAR THIS KID'S A SCRAPPER!

1-0 LOSS
18-INNING LOSS
TODAY HE'S TAKING ON CHICAGO ON THE ROAD BUT TOMORROW HE'S BACK AT THE FENWAY NEIGHBORHOOD VS. THE SENATORS... AND WATCH THIS SCRAPPER!!! SCRAP!
EDDIE GERMANO
BROCKTON ENTERPRISE 4/18/67

YA GOTTA HAVE HEART

HOW SWEET IT IS
A YEAR AGO JUST ABOUT EVERYONE HE CAME IN CONTACT WITH PASSED HIM BY... ESPECIALLY THE OTHER AL. CLUBS...
GUESS NOBODY LOVES A LOSER!
RED SOX
SPLAT
...BUT THIS IS 1967 AND OUR HERO'S RIDING HIGH BOTH IN THE STANDINGS AND AT THE GATE.
EASY, BACK THERE, DON'T GET CARELESS
SOX
BUT HE ISN'T SUPPOSED TO BE UP THERE!
1st DIVISION
2ND. DIV. CLUBS
EDDIE GERMANO

MASTER PLUMBER
HELP!
RED SOX
WHENEVER THE RED SOX PLUMBING HAS SPRUNG A LEAK THIS SEASON...
...ALONG COMES ACE STOPPER JIM LONBORG TO PLUG THE GAP. I HATE TO THINK WHERE THE FENWAY GANG WOULD BE WITHOUT HIM
A WRENCH IN TIME SAVES NINE!
EDDIE GERMANO

ONE OF A KIND
THE EXCITING RED SOX HAVE BEEN HOVERING OVER THOSE TOUGH ONE-RUN GAMES... THEY FELL TWICE IN THE BRIER BUSH AT MINNESOTA AND ONCE IN THE SOFT HAY OF VICTORY TO START THE CURRENT ROAD TRIP...
OOPS! OOPS!
RED SOX
1 RUN GAMES
...WE HOPE THE WILLIAMSMEN WILL BREAK INTO A HITTING SPREE AT KC TONIGHT TO SUPPORT THE PITCHING DEPT., WHICH HAS BEEN TOP-NOTCH OF LATE
EDDIE GERMANO

BE IT EVER SO HUMBLE

NO ROAD MAP NEEDED

THE **RED SOX** OPEN UP A KEY ROAD TRIP TONIGHT IN MINNESOTA AND TO CALL THE JUNKET "CRUCIAL" IS PUTTING IT MILDLY!

BATTING POWER

BOSTON

PITCHING ?

MINNESOTA

KANSAS CITY

CAL.

CRUCIAL

WE'LL KNOW WHAT OUR PENNANT CHANCES ARE AFTER THIS ONE!

EDDIE GERMANO
BROCKTON ENTERPRISE 8/4/67

WHAT'S TH' MATTER? YOU'RE SCREAMIN'
WHAT A NIGHTMARE, TH' SOX LOST!
WITH THE RED SOX IN THE THICK OF THE PENNANT FIGHT, DREAMS CAN BE FAR FROM PLEASANT
WHERE'S TH' MAALOX?
TAKE THAT!
OUR ULCERS HAVE BEEN PUNTING ON EVERY PITCH
WHAT'S HE MEAN... YAZ TAGGED UP N' SCORED?
AND THE GALS, LOVE 'EM (MR WIFE INCLUDED) HAVE SHOWN AN INTEREST IN BASEBALL THAT IS BAFFLING
WHAT A TEAM!
THEY START PRO FOOTBALL TOO EARLY!
GO-GO RED SOX
HAVE YA NOTICED HOW MANY OF THE "BASEBALL IS DEAD CLUB" HAVE JUMPED ON THE BAND-WAGON?
?
WHY NOT, USE LONBORG IN RELIEF!
BUNT! BUNT!
PLAY FOR TH' BIG INNING!
DICK WILLIAMS... MAY BE THE MANAGER OF THE YEAR, BUT HE'S GETTIN' PLENTY OF ASSISTANCE
EDDIE GERMANO
BROCKTON ENTERPRISE 8/29/67

WE WON THE PENNANT!
RED SOX
I CAN'T BELIEVE IT! I CAN'T BELIEVE IT!
EDDIE GERMANO BROCKTON ENTERPRISE 10/2/67

YAZ
MVP
EDDIE GERMANO BROCKTON ENTERPRISE

BIRDS OF A FEATHER

GO TO IT FELLAS!
BASEBALL COMMISSIONER WILLIAM D. ECKERT, THREW OUT THE FIRST BALL
LOU BROCK LED OFF WITH A CLEAN HIT TO LEFT
FREE SEATS FOR THOSE WITH GUTS, BILLBOARD STYLE
OFF! TO A FLYIN' START!
GAME WAS HELD UP BY A FAN CLINGING ON LEFT FIELD FOUL POLE
HAPPINESS IS A PLACE CALLED HOME!
BROCK TALLIED CARDS' FIRST RUN ON MARIS' GROUNDER TO SCOTT
BUT PITCHERS DON'T HIT!
THOSE CARDS LOOKED LIKE A SOLID BALL CLUB AND DESERVE THE FAVORITES' ROLL
GAME #1 IN THE RECORD
I'LL TAKE THAT!
JOSE SANTIAGO
IN ADDITION TO PITCHING A COURAGEOUS GAME, HIT A HOMER TO TIE THE SCORE AT 1-1 IN THE 3RD
THEY'LL BE WILD IN PUERTO RICO!
..HOWEVER, ADVERSARY
BOB GIBSON
WAS TRULY SUPERB IN CHUCKING HIS MATES TO THE LEADOFF WIN IN THE SERIES
YAZ!
MADE TWO DEFENSIVE GEMS...GREAT CATCH ON FLOOD AND THREW OUT JAVIER AT THE PLATE ON A PERFECT STRIKE
A DIFFERENT BREED OF CAT GO TO BASEBALL GAMES THESE DAYS AND THEY WERE MINI-MIZED LIKE RED SOX BATTERS
HEY!
RED SOX
GATE-B
AMAZING THE NUMBER OF FANS MILLING AROUND FENWAY WITHOUT TICKETS HOPING SOMEHOW TO GET IN
A MIRACLE MAYBE!
I KEEP FALLIN' IN!
THE BIRDS KEPT SANTIAGO IN A HOLE BY GETTING THEIR LEAD MAN ON BASE INNING AFTER INNING
THE CARDS STILL RUN BASES IN THE TRADITION OF PEPPER MARTIN OF ST. LOUIS "GAS HOUSE" FAME
MIKE SHANNON
SCOTTIE SOLVED GIBSON FOR A SINGLE AND DOUBLE FOR TWO OF THE SIX SOX HITS
C'MERE!
ELLY HOWARD'S NICE STOP ON A DIRT-SKIMMER
TODAY'S ANOTHER DAY AND JIM LONBORG WILL EVEN IT UP!
REDBIRD LOU BROCK! STOLE THE SHOW AND THE GAME WITH TWO STOLEN BASES, A PERFECT DAY AT THE PLATE AND SCORED HIS TEAM'S RUNS
WE HATE TO SAY IT BUT... HARRELSON LET A BALL DROP IN THAT SORELY-MISSED TONY C. WOULD'VE PUT IN HIS HIP POCKET
JUICE ANYONE?
CARDS USE AN ORANGE BALL FOR INFIELD PRACTICE
EDDIE GERMANO AT FENWAY PARK

WE WERE T'GETHER IN '46, TOO
AMERICAN LEAGUE PRESIDENT JOE CRONIN THREW OUT THE FIRST BALL AND INSISTED BOBBY DOERR STAY WITH HIM
GO-GO GO-GO
EDDIE BRESSOUD
JACK LAMABE
WED'S CROWD WAS SUBDUED BUT NOT SO YESTERDAY... WOW!
A COUPLE OF OL' SOX GOT IN THE GAME
YAZ DIDN'T HAVE A CHANCE TO GRAB JAVIER'S DOUBLE WHICH WOULD'VE SAVED LONBORG'S NO-HITTER
HALL OF FAME
ASPIRINS!
CHIRP CHIRP
RED SOX
JIM LONBORG STOOD ON THE HALL OF FAME THRESHOLD AS HE HAD THE ST. LOUIS BIRD EATING OUT OF HIS HAND BY FLINGING A NEAT ONE-HITTER
GO RED SOX
AGAIN! THOSE GUTSY BILL-BOARD CLINGERS
YAZ!
POW!
YES FOLKS, "IT'S THE YEAR OF THE YAZ!" WITH TWO SWINGS OF HIS MIGHTY HOME RUN BAT, HE PRESENTED THE RED SOX WITH MORE THAN ENOUGH RUNS TO EVEN THE SERIES
CHATTED WITH BALT. SPORTSWRITER JOHN STEADMAN WHO WAS A CATCHER ON THE 1944 BALT. LEGION TEAM VS. BROCKTON... HE SAYS "HELLO" TO THE COLOMBOS, EDNA McNEILL AND MARY CLARK
JERRY ADAIR ON BROCK ROCKED OL' FENWAY
JULIAN JAVIER'S SPECTACULAR PLAY ON HOWARD COST THE SOX A RUN AND MAYBE MORE
I MAY START A TIDE!
CURT FLOOD WAS THE FIRST CARDINAL TO REACH IN THE 7th VIA A FREE PASS
PASS
NL UMPIRE AL BARLICK, CALLS 'EM IN OPERATIC STYLE
"STEEEERIKE!"
RICO'S GREAT STOP ON CEPEDA IN THE 7th, SAVED THE NO-HITTER UP TO THAT POINT
DALTON JONES HAD A PAIR
BY THE TIME YOU READ THIS WE'LL BE JETTING TO ST. LOUIS... SEE YA MONDAY IN THE ENTERPRISE!
WE THOUGHT CEPEDA'S HIGH SKYER HIT THE CLOUDS AND DARNED IF IT DIDN'T RAIN ALMOST PRONTO
EDDIE GERMANO AT FENWAY PARK 10/6/67

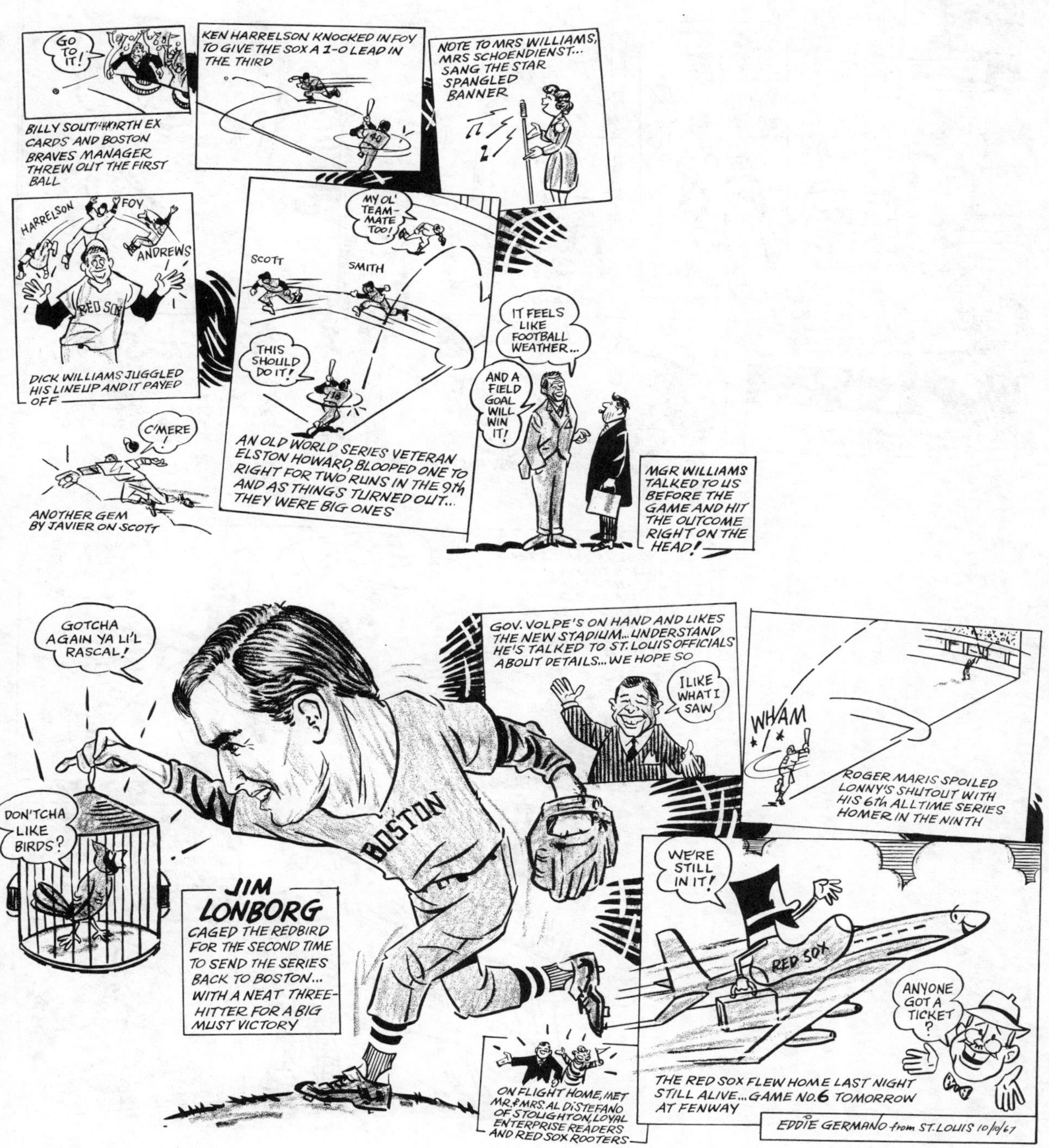
GO TO IT!
BILLY SOUTHWORTH EX CARDS AND BOSTON BRAVES MANAGER THREW OUT THE FIRST BALL
KEN HARRELSON KNOCKED IN FOY TO GIVE THE SOX A 1-0 LEAD IN THE THIRD
NOTE TO MRS WILLIAMS, MRS SCHOENDIENST... SANG THE STAR SPANGLED BANNER
HARRELSON
FOY
ANDREWS
RED SOX
DICK WILLIAMS JUGGLED HIS LINEUP AND IT PAYED OFF
MY OL' TEAM-MATE TOO!
SCOTT
SMITH
THIS SHOULD DO IT!
AN OLD WORLD SERIES VETERAN ELSTON HOWARD, BLOOPED ONE TO RIGHT FOR TWO RUNS IN THE 9th AND AS THINGS TURNED OUT... THEY WERE BIG ONES
IT FEELS LIKE FOOTBALL WEATHER...
AND A FIELD GOAL WILL WIN IT!
MGR WILLIAMS TALKED TO US BEFORE THE GAME AND HIT THE OUTCOME RIGHT ON THE HEAD!
C'MERE!
ANOTHER GEM BY JAVIER ON SCOTT
GOTCHA AGAIN YA LI'L RASCAL!
DON'TCHA LIKE BIRDS?
BOSTON
JIM LONBORG
CAGED THE REDBIRD FOR THE SECOND TIME TO SEND THE SERIES BACK TO BOSTON... WITH A NEAT THREE-HITTER FOR A BIG MUST VICTORY
GOV. VOLPE'S ON HAND AND LIKES THE NEW STADIUM... UNDERSTAND HE'S TALKED TO ST. LOUIS OFFICIALS ABOUT DETAILS... WE HOPE SO
I LIKE WHAT I SAW
WHAM
ROGER MARIS SPOILED LONNY'S SHUTOUT WITH HIS 6th ALLTIME SERIES HOMER IN THE NINTH
WE'RE STILL IN IT!
RED SOX
ANYONE GOT A TICKET?
ON FLIGHT HOME, MET MR.&MRS. AL DiSTEFANO OF STOUGHTON, LOYAL ENTERPRISE READERS AND RED SOX ROOTERS
THE RED SOX FLEW HOME LAST NIGHT STILL ALIVE... GAME NO. 6 TOMORROW AT FENWAY
EDDIE GERMANO from ST. LOUIS 10/10/67

NO TIME FOR TEARS

1968-1974

The seasons following the Impossible Dream were rife with might-have-beens. The Sox stayed in contention every year, but they failed to grab the top spot. Excellent individual performances brought opportunities that the team as a whole could not exploit. Nevertheless, every spring hope welled up in the hearts of loyal fans.

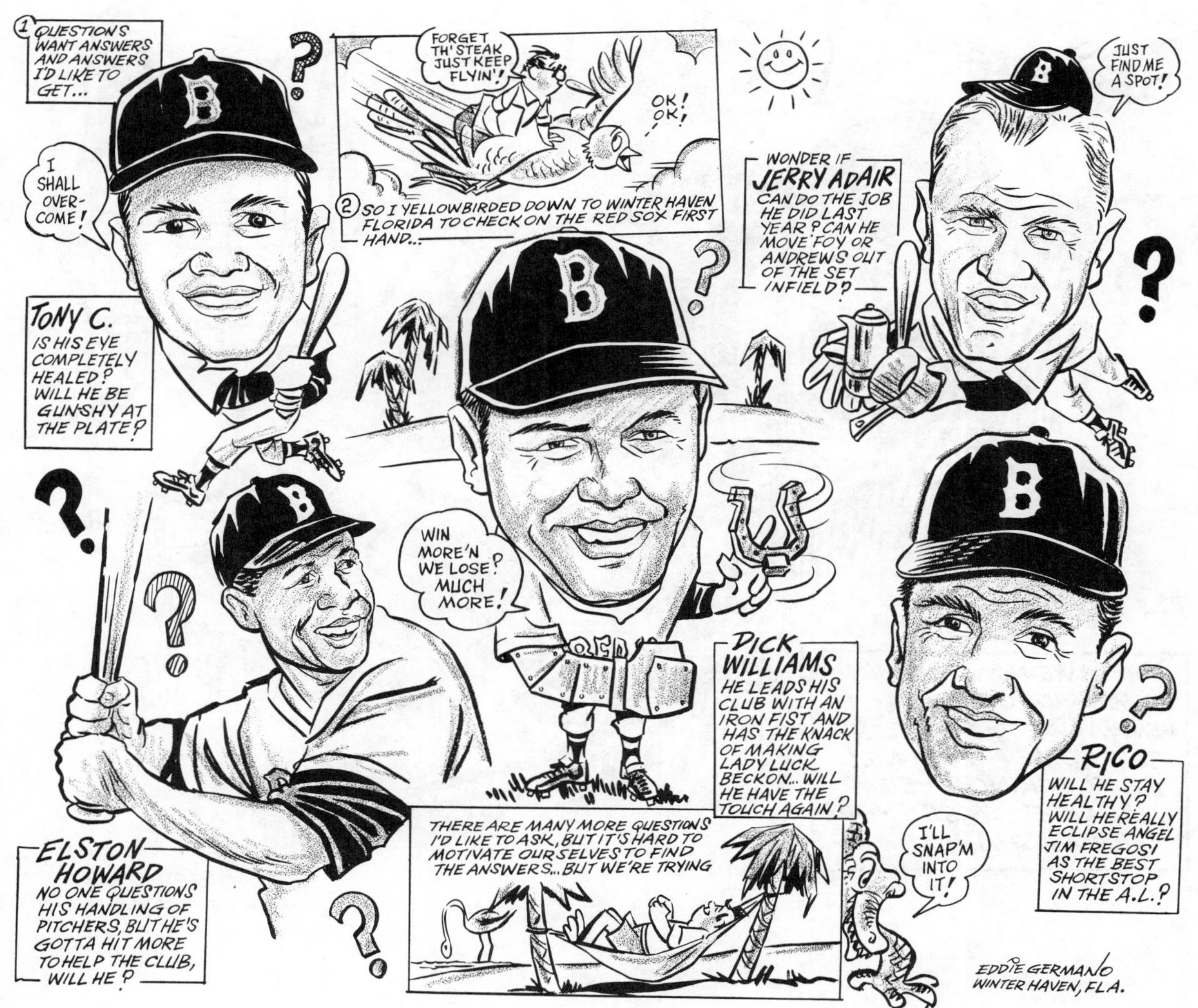

SHOE-IN!
I'VE GOT A COUPLE OF HOLES THIS YEAR, DARN IT!
NEVER MIND... IF THE SHOE FITS... WEAR IT!
RED SOX
TONY C.
LONBORG
1968 PENNANT
THE AMERICAN LEAGUE CHAMPIONS OPEN AT FENWAY VS. DETROIT AND THE HOME FOLKS WILL BE FLOCKING OVER THIS WEEK TO SEE HOW THINGS SHAPE UP
EDDIE GERMANO
BROCKTON ENTERPRISE 4/15/68

1
JIM LONBORG
TO TAKE UP SKIING FOR OFF SEASON CONDITIONING... (NEWS ITEM OF A FEW WEEKS AGO)
2
WHAT! WHY NOT BULL FIGHTIN'...
OR SKY DIVIN'... OR ALLIGATOR RASSLIN'...
OR AUTO RACIN'... OR EVEN RUSSIAN ROULETTE?
TO BE SURE, THE REACTION WAS ONE OF UTMOST APPREHENSION TO SAY THE LEAST
3
WHY, IT'S JUST LIKE COMING OFF THE MOUND
MEANWHILE JIM HILLED AND DALED...
4
OOPS!
...WHEN SUDDENLY, THE LEFT KNEE FAILED
5
OH MY GOODNESS, I KNEW THIS WOULD HAPPEN!
I'D BETTER GO SEE A FRIEND OF MINE AND FAST!
6
?
I KNOW IT'S IMPOSIN' BUT COULD YA MAKE A RETURN TRIP 'N PICK UP THOSE *!! SKIS YA LEFT FER LONNY?
EDDIE GERMANO BROCKTON ENTERPRISE 12/27/67

JOE LAHOUD
THE YOUNGSTER HAS LOOKED GOOD ESPECIALLY AT BAT, THE TALK HERE IS WITH MORE SEASONING HE'LL MAKE IT SOON
THIS BEING HURRICANE COUNTRY, IT'S WINDY ENOUGH AT TIMES TO SHAKE THE LIGHT TOWERS AT THE BALL PARK
EX PHIL... GENE OLIVER... THE VETERAN CATCHER IS A DEFINITE LONG BALL THREAT, WILL BE HELPFUL IN PINCH-HITTING ROLES
WINTER HAVEN
ON MOST EVERY STREET CORNER, YOU'LL SEE COIN-OPERATED MACHINES WHERE NEWSPAPERS CAN BE BOUGHT
WONDER WHAT THEY'RE UP TO?
OK FELLAS!
RED SOX
MANAGER DICK WILLIAMS HOLDS A PRESS POW-WOW AFTER EACH GAME, EVEN THOUGH EXHIBITION GAMES DON'T COUNT, HE'S NOT PLEASANT WHEN HIS TEAM LOSES
THINK I'LL QUIT
50¢
THE NATIVES ARE CONCERNED ABOUT TAXES HERE TOO, A PACK OF CIGARETTES WILL COST FIFTY CENTS STARTING ON APRIL 1st
GOTCHA!
GOTCHA !!!
RED SOX EQUIPMENT MANAGER... DON FITZPATRICK AND REGGIE SMITH PLAYING COWBOY, OUTSIDE OUR MOTEL ROOM WITH TOY PISTOLS
IT LOOKS TO US THAT YAZ IS STANDING A LITTLE CLOSER TO THE PLATE AND DON'T BE SURPRISED IF OTHER TEAMS PULL DEFENSIVE SHIFTS ON HIM NOW THAT THE WHITE SOX HAVE STARTED IT
EDDIE GERMANO
WINTER HAVEN, FLORIDA

THE RED SOX PENNANT VINTAGE (ONE YEAR OLD) HAS BEEN TIPPED OVER BY OF ALL PEOPLE, THE OAKLAND A'S...
A CORK IN TIMES SAVES OUR NINE!
...TONIGHT IN WASHINGTON, JOSE SANTIAGO (WINNER OF THREE STRAIGHT) WILL BE OUT WITH THE STOPPER BEFORE EVERYTHING SPILLS ON THE BASEMENT FLOOR OF THE A.L.
EDDIE GERMANO
BROCKTON ENTERPRISE 5/7/68

YOU'LL RECALL DICK WILLIAMS' OPENED THE SEASON WITH DALTON JONES AT 3RD BASE LEAVING JOE BROODING ON THE BENCH
I CAN SAY THINGS BUT I WON'T
JOE FOY...
ONCE HE CRACKED THE LINEUP, HE PROCEEDED TO NAIL DOWN THE HOT CORNER SACK WITH A VENGEANCE... GOING INTO TONIGHT'S GAME WITH THE TWINS JOE'S HITTING AT A .293 CLIP
WHAM
HIS FIELDING HAS BEEN FOY-BULOUS TOO!
THE RED SOX ARE IN JUST ABOUT THE SAME POSITION AS A YEAR AGO IN THE STANDINGS, IF JOE STAYS HOT, THING'S'LL BE LOOKING UP FROM HERE ON!
EDDIE GERMANO
BROCKTON ENTERPRISE 5/24/68

I'LL GET KILT!
RED SOX
WHEN I SAW GARY IN SPRING TRAINING HIS EARS WERE RINGING FROM THE POUNDING HE TOOK FROM ENEMY HITTERS
GARY BELL
B
BONG
GONG
TH' BELL'S RINGIN' FOR ME'N MY PALS
...THESE DAYS GARY'S DOING HIS OWN RINGING WITH A 4-1 RECORD INCLUDING A PAIR OF SHUTOUTS... CONTROL AND A SNAPPING CURVE HAVE SUPPLEMENTED HIS FAST BALL WHICH HAS LOST SOME OF THE OL' HUM
EDDIE GERMANO
BROCKTON ENTERPRISE 6/4/68

WITH THE RED SOX WELL IN ARREARS OF FIRST PLACE MANY QUARTERS ARE MAKING MANAGER DICK WILLIAMS THE CHIEF TARGET...
HOLD IT! LET'S LOOK AT A FEW FACTS
INJURY TO TONY C., LONBORG'S SKIING ACCIDENT, AN OFF YEAR & AN INJURY TO YAZ, SORE ARMS ON THE PITCHING STAFF SCOTT'S BATTING SLUMP VARIOUS OTHER INJURIES ETC... ETC...
... ON OCCASIONS, DICK HAS SHOWN A LITTLE LESS OF HIS 1967 GENIUS BUT THIS CORNER FEELS THE FAULT OF THE BOSOX PLIGHT DOESN'T LIE WITH THE MANAGER... OUR FACT SHEET BEARS THIS OUT
EDDIE GERMANO 8/2/68

1969

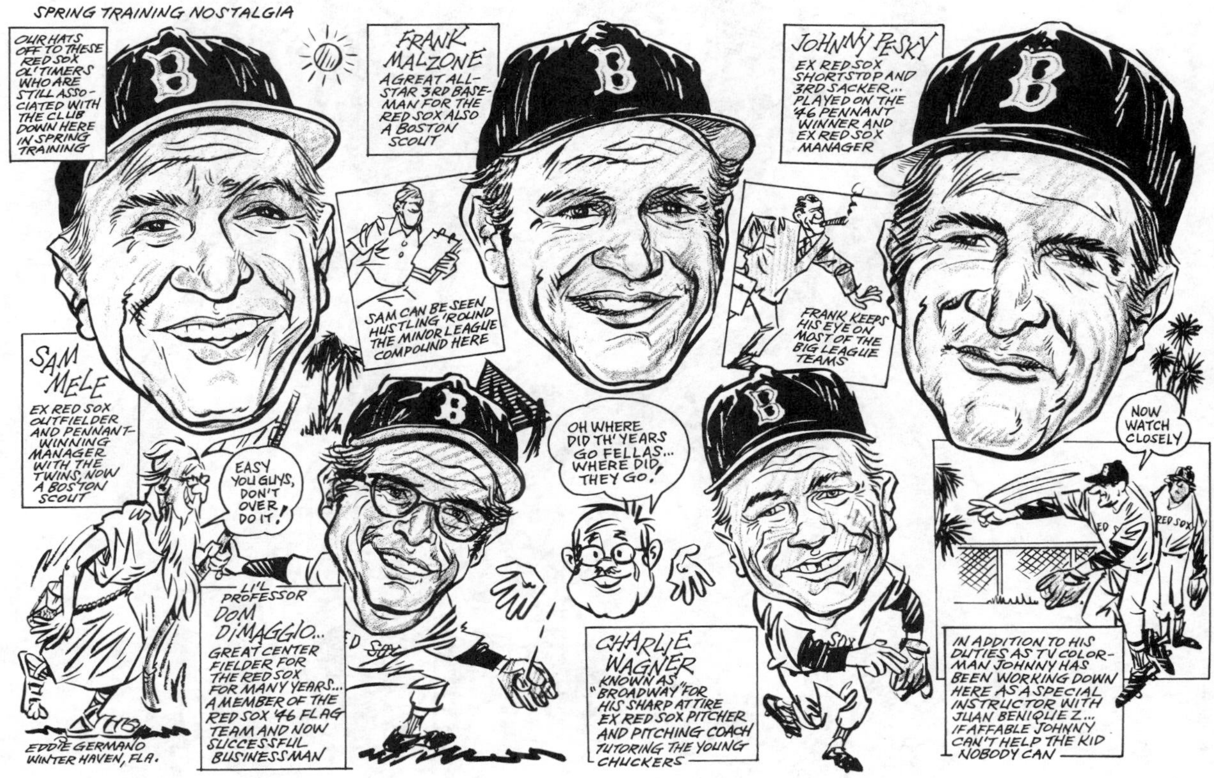

SPRING TRAINING NOSTALGIA
OUR HATS OFF TO THESE RED SOX OL'TIMERS WHO ARE STILL ASSOCIATED WITH THE CLUB DOWN HERE IN SPRING TRAINING
FRANK MALZONE
A GREAT ALL-STAR 3RD BASEMAN FOR THE RED SOX ALSO A BOSTON SCOUT
JOHNNY PESKY
EX RED SOX SHORTSTOP AND 3RD SACKER... PLAYED ON THE '46 PENNANT WINNER AND EX RED SOX MANAGER
SAM CAN BE SEEN HUSTLING 'ROUND THE MINOR LEAGUE COMPOUND HERE
FRANK KEEPS HIS EYE ON MOST OF THE BIG LEAGUE TEAMS
SAM MELE
EX RED SOX OUTFIELDER AND PENNANT-WINNING MANAGER WITH THE TWINS, NOW A BOSTON SCOUT
EASY YOU GUYS, DON'T OVER DO IT!
OH WHERE DID TH' YEARS GO FELLAS... WHERE DID THEY GO!
NOW WATCH CLOSELY
LI'L PROFESSOR DOM DiMAGGIO... GREAT CENTER FIELDER FOR THE RED SOX FOR MANY YEARS... A MEMBER OF THE RED SOX '46 FLAG TEAM AND NOW SUCCESSFUL BUSINESSMAN
CHARLIE WAGNER
KNOWN AS "BROADWAY" FOR HIS SHARP ATTIRE EX RED SOX PITCHER AND PITCHING COACH TUTORING THE YOUNG CHUCKERS
IN ADDITION TO HIS DUTIES AS TV COLORMAN JOHNNY HAS BEEN WORKING DOWN HERE AS A SPECIAL INSTRUCTOR WITH JUAN BENIQUEZ... IF AFFABLE JOHNNY CAN'T HELP THE KID NOBODY CAN
EDDIE GERMANO
WINTER HAVEN, FLA.

HANG IN THERE!
FROM OUR VANTAGE POINT LOOKING AT THE YOUNG SEASON, IT'S EASY TO SEE WHAT THE BIG QUESTION IS REGARDING RED SOX CHANCES IN 1969...
PITCHING
?
RED SOX
LET'S HANG IN THERE !
WILL IT HOLD UP?
EDDIE GERMANO 4/23/69

THOUGH THINGS HAVEN'T BEEN GOING RIGHT FOR THE RED SOX OF LATE... A BRIGHT SPOT HAS BEEN THE HITTING OF TONY C., WHO HAS RIPPED SIX HR'S IN THE PAST WEEK AND MOST OF THEM CLUTCH JOBS

BOOM
POW
WHAM
BANG
SOCK

AND IF ANYONE STILL HAS ANY DOUBTS 'BOUT'M, FORGET IT!.. THIS KID'S BACK ALL TH' WAY!

EDDIE GERMANO
ENTERPRISE SPORTS

DICK SCHOFIELD HAS REALLY DONE IT ALL AS UTILITY MAN AND PINCH HITTER DELUXE FOR THE RED SOX
THEY CALL HIM "DUCKY" AND HE'S BEEN JUST THAT!
WHY, YER JUST A LI'L HALF PINT!
DICK'S THE LITTLE SCRAPPY TYPE WHO CAN PLAY MOST OF THE INFIELD POSITIONS QUITE ADEQUATELY... HE'S BEEN DOING A GREAT JOB FILLING IN FOR THE INJURED MIKE ANDREWS BOTH IN THE FIELD AND AT THE PLATE
PUT ME DOWN OR I'LL BELT YA!
I'M NOT QUITE SO DARIN'!
DICK'S REPLACED THE HAWK AS THE RED SOX MOD-STYLE DRESSER
EDDIE GERMANO 6/5/69
1 THE RED SOX HAVE NO LESS THAN THREE EX BIG LEAGUE MANAGERS ON THEIR PAYROLL WITH AT LEAST TWO (MELE AND PESKY) ITCHING TO GET BACK INTO PILOTING AGAIN...
HAYWOOD SULLIVAN
SAM MELE
JOHNNY PESKY
2 ...AND WITH THE CLUB FLOUNDERING, IT'S MORE THAN THE HUMIDITY THAT'S MAKING IT STICKY FOR DICK WILLIAMS THESE DAYS...
3 ...HOWEVER, IT'S OUR THINKING THAT IT'S NOT ENTIRELY THE MANAGER'S FAULT, POOR PITCHING, CATCHING, INJURIES PLUS A MEDIOCRE YEAR BY YAZ HAVE CONTRIBUTED HEAVILY TO THE CURRENT PLIGHT OF THE TEAM
EDDIE GERMANO ENTERPRISE SPORTS 8/7/69

A New Hose for the Hose!
LAST NIGHT THE RED SOX INTRODUCED THEIR NEW MANAGER TO THE PRESS...
TORONTO
1967
TWO STRAIGHT CHAMPIONSHIPS
...AND TO NO ONE'S SURPRISE, DICK WILLIAMS CAME INTO HIS NEW OFFICE WELL EQUIPPED TO TAKE OVER
HIGGINS
PESKY
HERMAN
THE HOT SEAT
EDDIE GERMANO AT FENWAY PARK
BACK ON SEPT. 29, 1966 I DREW THIS CARTOON WHEN DICK WILLIAMS WAS MADE MANAGER OF THE RED SOX...
MANAGER
...AND FROM WHERE I STAND, THE MANAGER'S CHAIR IS STILL FLAMING!
SO, TO THE NEW RED SOX MANAGER WHOEVER YOU MAY BE... BEST OF LUCK AND COME EQUIPPED WITH A FIRE BUCKET!
EDDIE GERMANO
ENTERPRISE SPORTS
9/25/69

1970

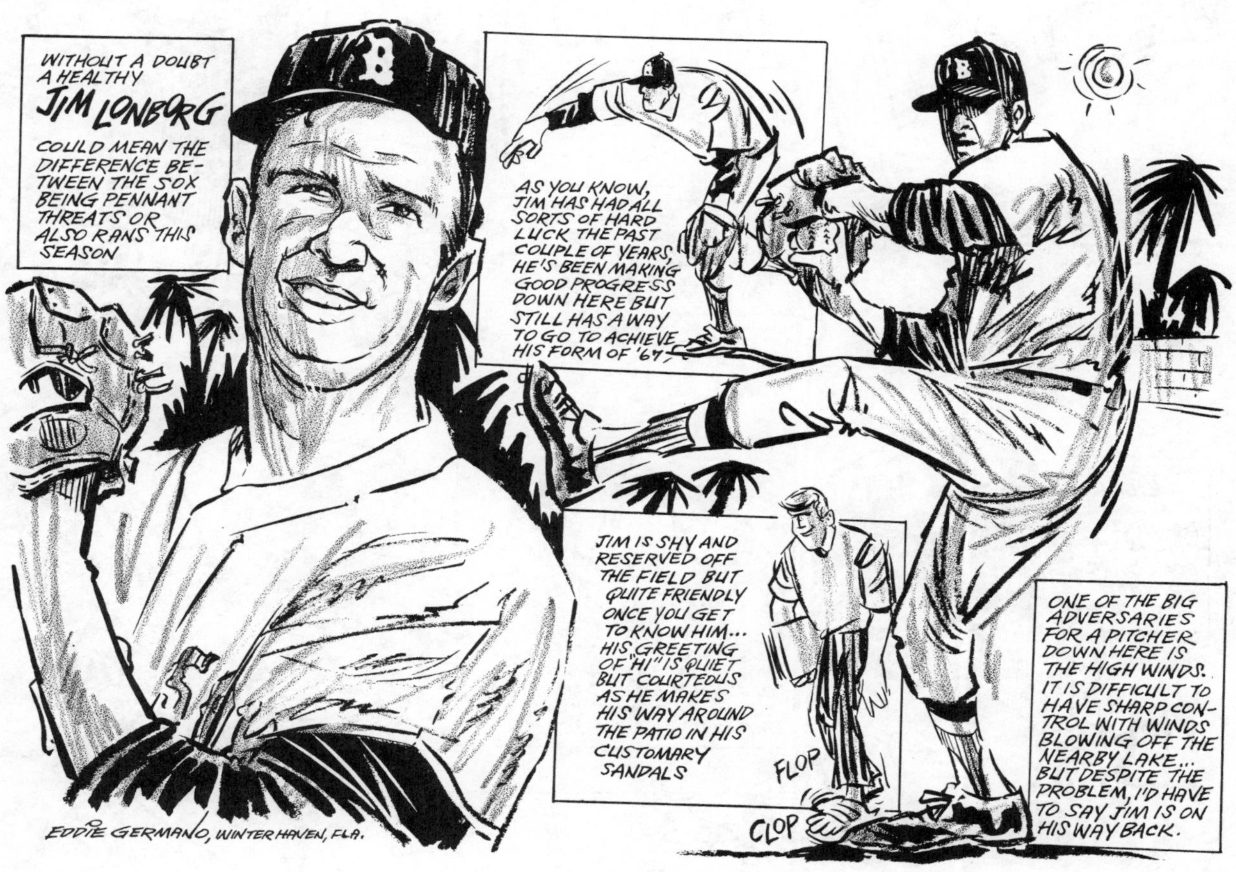

WITHOUT A DOUBT A HEALTHY
JIM LONBORG
COULD MEAN THE DIFFERENCE BETWEEN THE SOX BEING PENNANT THREATS OR ALSO RANS THIS SEASON
AS YOU KNOW, JIM HAS HAD ALL SORTS OF HARD LUCK THE PAST COUPLE OF YEARS. HE'S BEEN MAKING GOOD PROGRESS DOWN HERE BUT STILL HAS A WAY TO GO TO ACHIEVE HIS FORM OF '67.
JIM IS SHY AND RESERVED OFF THE FIELD BUT QUITE FRIENDLY ONCE YOU GET TO KNOW HIM... HIS GREETING OF "HI" IS QUIET BUT COURTEOUS AS HE MAKES HIS WAY AROUND THE PATIO IN HIS CUSTOMARY SANDALS
FLOP
CLOP
ONE OF THE BIG ADVERSARIES FOR A PITCHER DOWN HERE IS THE HIGH WINDS. IT IS DIFFICULT TO HAVE SHARP CONTROL WITH WINDS BLOWING OFF THE NEARBY LAKE... BUT DESPITE THE PROBLEM, I'D HAVE TO SAY JIM IS ON HIS WAY BACK.
EDDIE GERMANO, WINTER HAVEN, FLA.

WITH THE WINTER MEETINGS CONCLUDED, IT WAS DISAPPOINTING TO FIND **MA RED SOX** HANGING OUT THE SAME OL' WASH

27 SONNY SIEBERT... ARM OPERATION

21 RAY CULP... SORE ARM PROBLEMS

16 JIM LONBORG... ARM TROUBLE, GENERAL PHYSICAL AILMENTS

30 JOSE SANTIAGO... ARM OPERATION

15 MIKE NAGY... BACK PROBLEMS

FROM WHERE I SIT, THINGS LOOK MIGHTY GOOD AT MOST EVERY POSITION, BUT THE PITCHING LEAVES ME HANGING. GRANTED PITCHING IS HARD TO COME BY THESE DAYS BUT IF **MA** DOESN'T GET SOME NEW ARMS... YOU CAN FORGET ABOUT NEXT YEAR EVEN BEFORE IT STARTS!

EDDIE GERMANO
ENTERPRISE SPORTS

ONE OF THE HIGHLIGHTS OF SPRING TRAINING 1970 IS THE CONIGLIARO BROTHER ACT...

BILLY

WITH YAZ IN LEFT AND REGGIE IN CENTER BILLY C. ISN'T GIVEN MUCH OF A CHANCE TO MAKE THE CLUB AS A REGULAR...

TONY

BUT, IF BROTHER TONY SHOULD FALTER IN RIGHT, BILLY COULD FIND HIS SLOT THERE...

TH'CONIGS HAVE THEIR OWN ROOTIN' SECTION DOWN HERE FROM PAPA C. ON DOWN!

...YOUNG BILL HAS ALL THE TOOLS WITH THE EXCEPTION OF TONY'S POWER... DURING THE FINAL MONTH OF THE '69 SEASON TONY HIT .315 AND FINISHED UP WITH 20 HOMERS TO CAP OFF HIS COMEBACK

BOTH BOYS LOOK IN FINE SHAPE AND HELP TO GIVE THE RED SOX ONE OF THE BEST OUTFIELDS IN BASEBALL

EDDIE GERMANO
WINTER HAVEN, FLA.

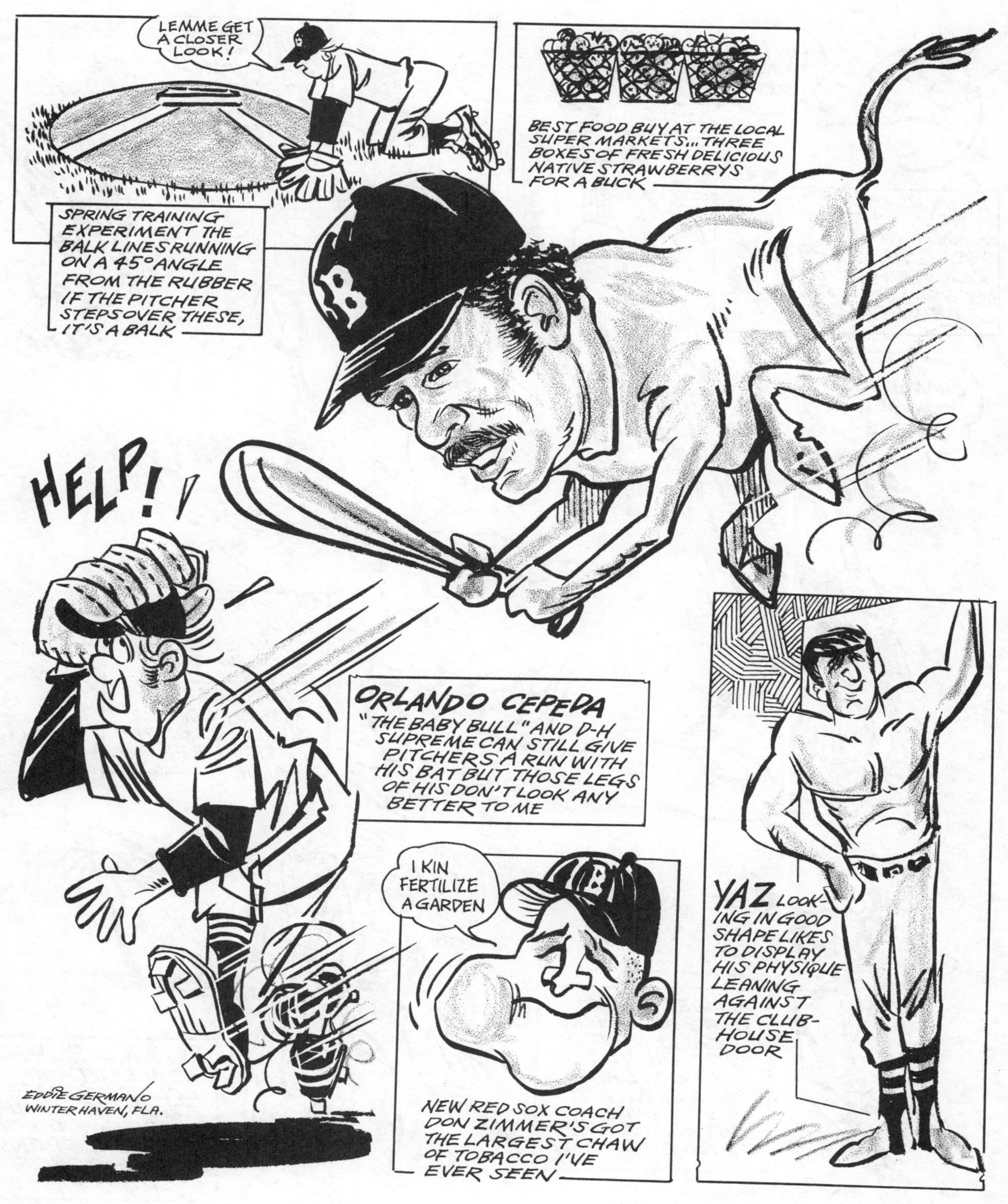
LEMME GET A CLOSER LOOK!
SPRING TRAINING EXPERIMENT THE BALK LINES RUNNING ON A 45° ANGLE FROM THE RUBBER IF THE PITCHER STEPS OVER THESE, IT'S A BALK
BEST FOOD BUY AT THE LOCAL SUPER MARKETS... THREE BOXES OF FRESH DELICIOUS NATIVE STRAWBERRYS FOR A BUCK
HELP!!
ORLANDO CEPEDA
"THE BABY BULL" AND D-H SUPREME CAN STILL GIVE PITCHERS A RUN WITH HIS BAT BUT THOSE LEGS OF HIS DON'T LOOK ANY BETTER TO ME
I KIN FERTILIZE A GARDEN
NEW RED SOX COACH DON ZIMMER'S GOT THE LARGEST CHAW OF TOBACCO I'VE EVER SEEN
YAZ LOOKING IN GOOD SHAPE LIKES TO DISPLAY HIS PHYSIQUE LEANING AGAINST THE CLUBHOUSE DOOR
EDDIE GERMANO
WINTER HAVEN, FLA.

A LITTLE OF THIS... AND A LITTLE OF THAT

ARE YOU-ALL SURE ?
YOU-ALL RIGHT !
WAITRESSES DOWN HERE JUST WON'T ACCEPT THE FACT THAT I DON'T DIG HASHED-BROWN 'TATERS AND GRITS WITH MY BREAK-FAST
SLATED FOR A MINOR LEAGUE COACHING JOB... BIG BOB VEALE IS A PRO IN EVERY WAY WITH THE FANS
GEE JOE DiMAGGIO'S BROTHER !
THANKS KID !
MY NEXT DOOR NEIGHBOR AT THE HOTEL IS FORMER RED SOX OUTFIELDING GREAT DOM DiMAGGIO WHO STILL IS UNDER BROTHER JOE'S SHADOW
THE ART CRAZE HAS HIT HERE WITH A FLOURISH YOUR PROFILE CAN BE EMBELLISHED ALMOST EVERY-WHERE INCLUD-ING DISNEYWORLD AND CYPRESS GARDENS
RICK BURLESON
VIC CORRELL
BERNIE CARBO
I LIKE THESE GUYS FOR NO OTHER REASON THAN THE FACT THEY ARE THE HARD-NOSE TYPE WHO BATTLE FOR YOU ALL THE WAY
SOME OF OUR NORTHERN FRIENDS SHOULD KNOW BETTER

HIGH HOPES
I'M UP 'N AT 'EM!
RED SOX
PENNANT HOPES
THE RED SOX BLAST OFF THEIR 1970 SEASON TOMORROW FROM THE YANKEE STADIUM LAUNCHING PAD.. EDDIE KASKO'S GOT ALL SYSTEMS READY TO GO!!! BEST OF LUCK BOYS, SEE YA AT FENWAY NEXT TUESDAY
ZOOM
RED SOX
NEVER MIND WAIT 'TILL NEXT YEAR, THIS IS TH YEAR! (I HOPE)
PHIL PHAN
EDDIE GERMANO ENTERPRISE SPORTS
TRIAL BALLOON
LET'S FACE IT KIDS, THE 1970 RED SOX LOOK LIKE A FLAT BALL CLUB AND THE SHAME OF IT ALL IS THAT THIS TEAM IS LOADED WITH TALENT...
...OR A LI'L OL' FASHION WHIPPIN'... MAYBE, EDDIE?
...AND WHILE WE'RE STILL HOPEFUL THAT EDDIE KASKO CAN PUMP A LITTLE LIFE INTO THE DEFLATED FENWAY BALLOON, MAYBE ANOTHER WAY MIGHT HELP!
EDDIE GERMANO ENTERPRISE SPORTS
GETTIN' HIS KICKS
WHEN YOU LOOK BACK OVER THE FIRST HALF OF THE SEASON, IT'S SICKENING TO RECALL THE MANY GAMES KASKO'S BOYS KICKED AWAY WHICH THEY SHOULD'VE WON...
RED SOX
POW!
1st HALF
OH M'GOSH, THERE GOES ANOTHER!
...AND NOW, AS THE SOX MOVE INTO THE SECOND HALF OF THE 1970 CAMPAIGN, EACH STEP LOOMS MIGHTY IMPORTANT IF THEY EVER HOPE TO MAKE UP ANY GROUND...'CAUSE THIS IS IT BABY!
EASY DOES IT, NOW!
2ND HALF
EDDIE GERMANO ENTERPRISE SPORTS

THE IMPOSSIBLE NIGHTMARE
LOUISVILLE COLONELS
JIM LONBORG
JOSE SANTIAGO
LOUIS
LOUISV
PHIL PHAN
EDDIE GERMANO
ENTERPRISE SPORTS

1971

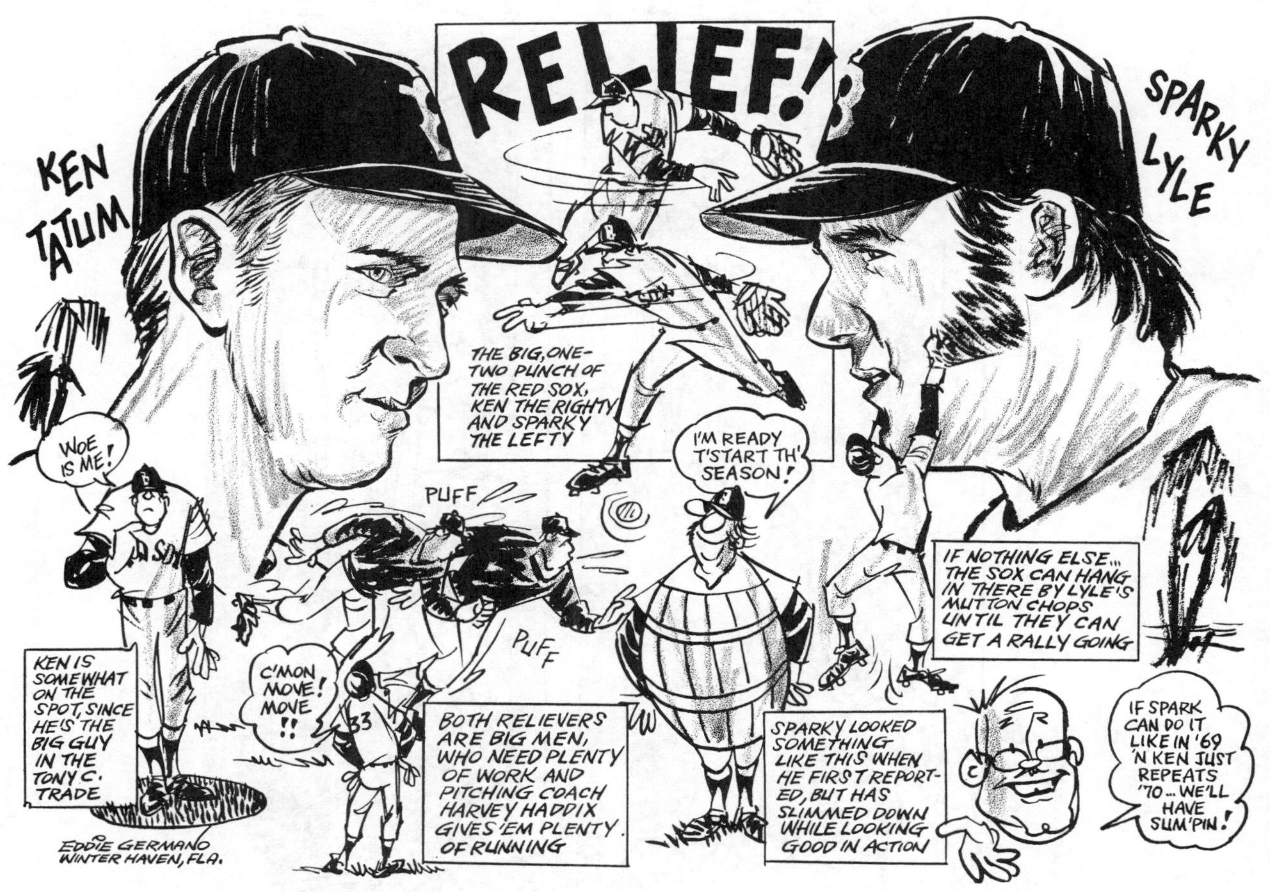

RELIEF!
KEN TATUM
SPARKY LYLE
THE BIG, ONE-TWO PUNCH OF THE RED SOX, KEN THE RIGHTY AND SPARKY THE LEFTY
WOE IS ME!
PUFF
I'M READY T'START TH' SEASON!
IF NOTHING ELSE... THE SOX CAN HANG IN THERE BY LYLE'S MUTTON CHOPS UNTIL THEY CAN GET A RALLY GOING
PUFF
KEN IS SOMEWHAT ON THE SPOT, SINCE HE'S THE BIG GUY IN THE TONY C. TRADE
C'MON MOVE! MOVE!!
BOTH RELIEVERS ARE BIG MEN, WHO NEED PLENTY OF WORK AND PITCHING COACH HARVEY HADDIX GIVES 'EM PLENTY OF RUNNING
SPARKY LOOKED SOMETHING LIKE THIS WHEN HE FIRST REPORTED, BUT HAS SLIMMED DOWN WHILE LOOKING GOOD IN ACTION
IF SPARK CAN DO IT LIKE IN '69 'N KEN JUST REPEATS '70... WE'LL HAVE SUM'PIN!
EDDIE GERMANO WINTER HAVEN, FLA.

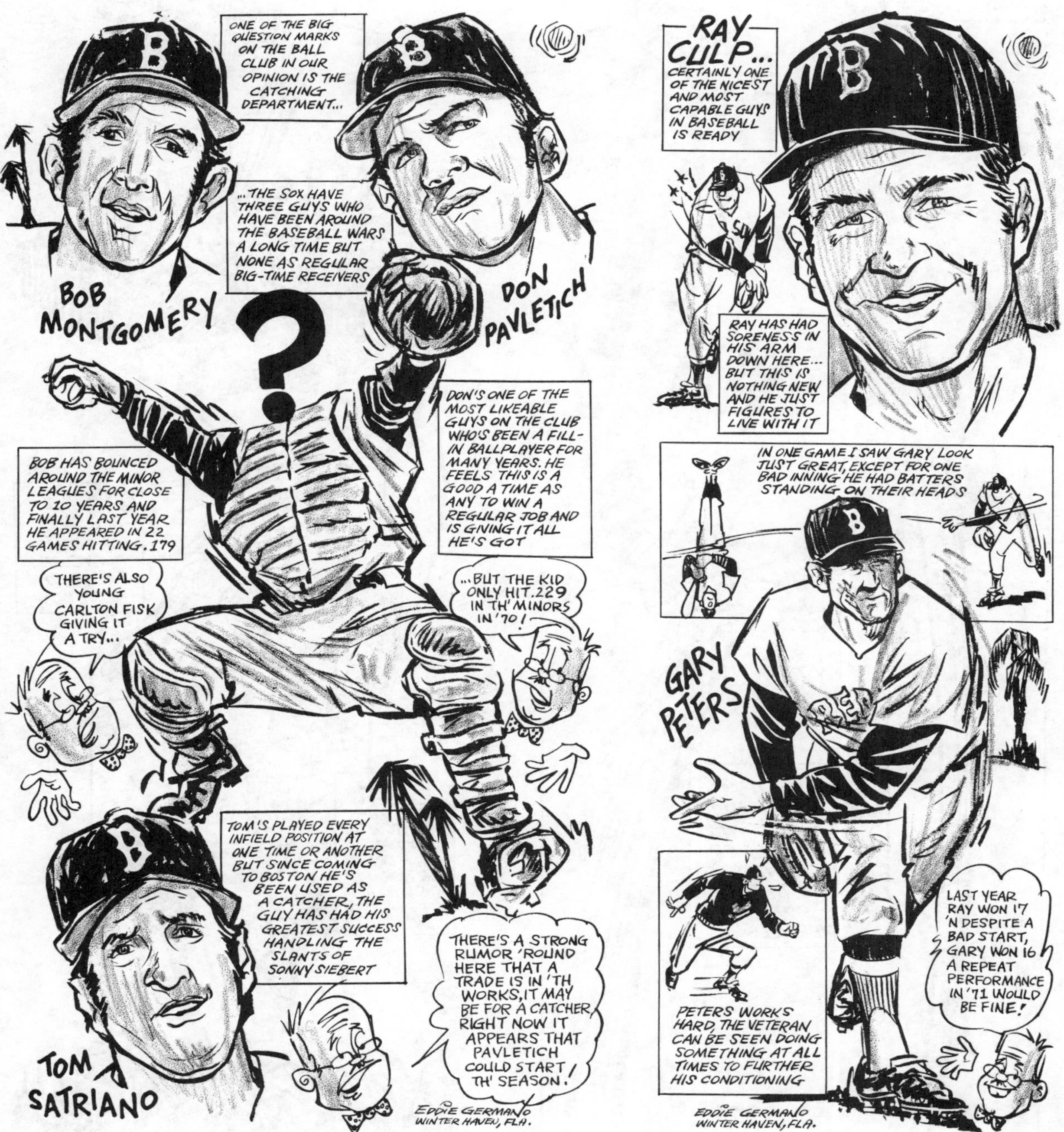

ONE OF THE BIG QUESTION MARKS ON THE BALL CLUB IN OUR OPINION IS THE CATCHING DEPARTMENT...
...THE SOX HAVE THREE GUYS WHO HAVE BEEN AROUND THE BASEBALL WARS A LONG TIME BUT NONE AS REGULAR BIG-TIME RECEIVERS
BOB MONTGOMERY
DON PAVLETICH
?
BOB HAS BOUNCED AROUND THE MINOR LEAGUES FOR CLOSE TO 10 YEARS AND FINALLY LAST YEAR HE APPEARED IN 22 GAMES HITTING .179
DON'S ONE OF THE MOST LIKEABLE GUYS ON THE CLUB WHO'S BEEN A FILL-IN BALLPLAYER FOR MANY YEARS. HE FEELS THIS IS A GOOD A TIME AS ANY TO WIN A REGULAR JOB AND IS GIVING IT ALL HE'S GOT
THERE'S ALSO YOUNG CARLTON FISK GIVING IT A TRY...
...BUT THE KID ONLY HIT .229 IN TH' MINORS IN '70!
TOM'S PLAYED EVERY INFIELD POSITION AT ONE TIME OR ANOTHER BUT SINCE COMING TO BOSTON HE'S BEEN USED AS A CATCHER, THE GUY HAS HAD HIS GREATEST SUCCESS HANDLING THE SLANTS OF SONNY SIEBERT
THERE'S A STRONG RUMOR 'ROUND HERE THAT A TRADE IS IN 'TH WORKS, IT MAY BE FOR A CATCHER, RIGHT NOW IT APPEARS THAT PAVLETICH COULD START TH' SEASON!
TOM SATRIANO
EDDIE GERMANO WINTER HAVEN, FLA.
RAY CULP... CERTAINLY ONE OF THE NICEST AND MOST CAPABLE GUYS IN BASEBALL IS READY
RAY HAS HAD SORENESS IN HIS ARM DOWN HERE... BUT THIS IS NOTHING NEW AND HE JUST FIGURES TO LIVE WITH IT
IN ONE GAME I SAW GARY LOOK JUST GREAT, EXCEPT FOR ONE BAD INNING HE HAD BATTERS STANDING ON THEIR HEADS
GARY PETERS
LAST YEAR RAY WON 17 'N DESPITE A BAD START, GARY WON 16 A REPEAT PERFORMANCE IN '71 WOULD BE FINE!
PETERS WORKS HARD, THE VETERAN CAN BE SEEN DOING SOMETHING AT ALL TIMES TO FURTHER HIS CONDITIONING
EDDIE GERMANO WINTER HAVEN, FLA.

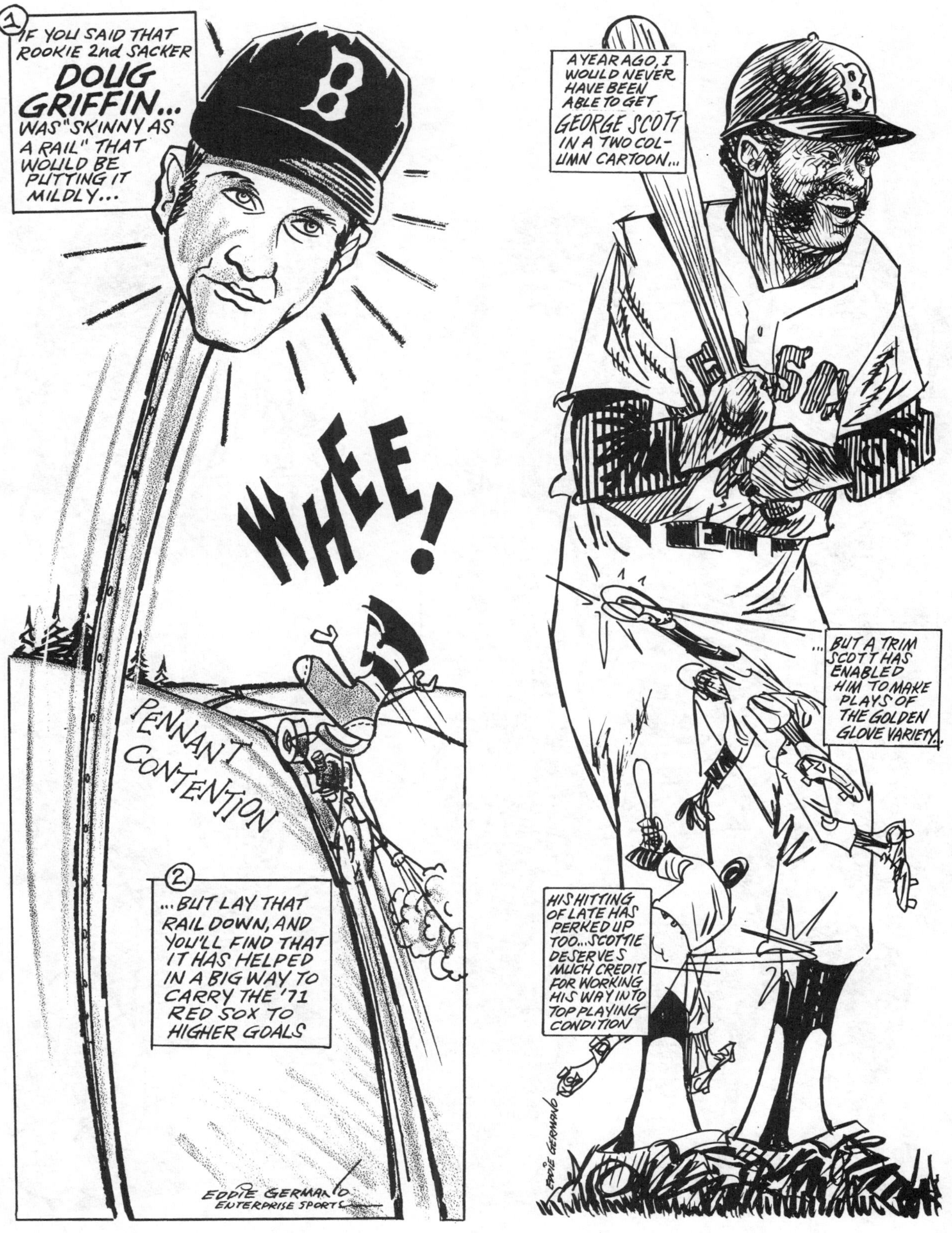

1 IF YOU SAID THAT ROOKIE 2nd SACKER DOUG GRIFFIN... WAS "SKINNY AS A RAIL" THAT WOULD BE PUTTING IT MILDLY...
WHEE!
PENNANT CONTENTION
2 ...BUT LAY THAT RAIL DOWN, AND YOU'LL FIND THAT IT HAS HELPED IN A BIG WAY TO CARRY THE '71 RED SOX TO HIGHER GOALS
EDDIE GERMANO
ENTERPRISE SPORTS
A YEAR AGO, I WOULD NEVER HAVE BEEN ABLE TO GET GEORGE SCOTT IN A TWO COLUMN CARTOON...
...BUT A TRIM SCOTT HAS ENABLED HIM TO MAKE PLAYS OF THE GOLDEN GLOVE VARIETY...
HIS HITTING OF LATE HAS PERKED UP TOO... SCOTTIE DESERVES MUCH CREDIT FOR WORKING HIS WAY INTO TOP PLAYING CONDITION
EDDIE GERMANO

IT SEEMS SUCH A SHORT TIME AGO THAT THE 1971 VERSION OF THE RED SOX WAS LOOKING LIKE THE JET SET WITH ALL ENGINES HUMMING A FIRST PLACE TUNE...
FLY ME TO TH' MOON
...'N LET ME PLAY
AMONG TH' STARS
... WHEN ALL OF A SUDDEN IT HAPPENED, ALMOST WITHOUT ANY WARNING...
PITCHING
MANAGING FLAWS
HITTING
DEFENSE
SOME-BODY DO SOMETHIN'!
DON'T WORRY, WE'LL THINK OF SOMETHIN'!
... BUT DON'T FRET FOLKS, WE HAVEN'T FALLEN THAT FAR DOWN AND WE STILL MAY ZOOM RIGHT UP ONCE AGAIN... RIGHT?
EDDIE GERMANO
ENTERPRISE SPORTS

JACK OF ALL TRADES
WHEN AN EMERGENCY COMES UP AND MANAGER EDDIE KASKO YELLS HELP! THE GUY YOU CAN DEPEND ON TO DO THE JOB IS... JOHN KENNEDY WHO IS FAST ESTABLISHING HIMSELF AS ONE OF THE TOP UTILITY PLAYERS IN BASEBALL
JUST TELL ME WHERE! 'N I'LL TAKE CARE OF IT!
MAYBE IT'S A GOOD OMEN... REMEMBER JERRY ADAIR IN '67!
EDDIE GERMANO ENTERPRISE SPORTS

1972

NOT ONLY HAVE CERTAIN PLAYERS ROCKED THE BOAT, SOME HAVE CAUSED IT TO CAPSIZE... AND ONE IMPORTANT SURVIVOR IS NONE OTHER THAN SKIPPER EDDIE KASKO.!!!
RED SOX
"NEW 1972 CONTRACT"
S.S. RED SOX
... WANNA BET SOME WILL NEVER MAKE IT ON BOARD ONCE THE STORM HAS SUBSIDED!
EDDIE GERMANO
ENTERPRISE SPORTS

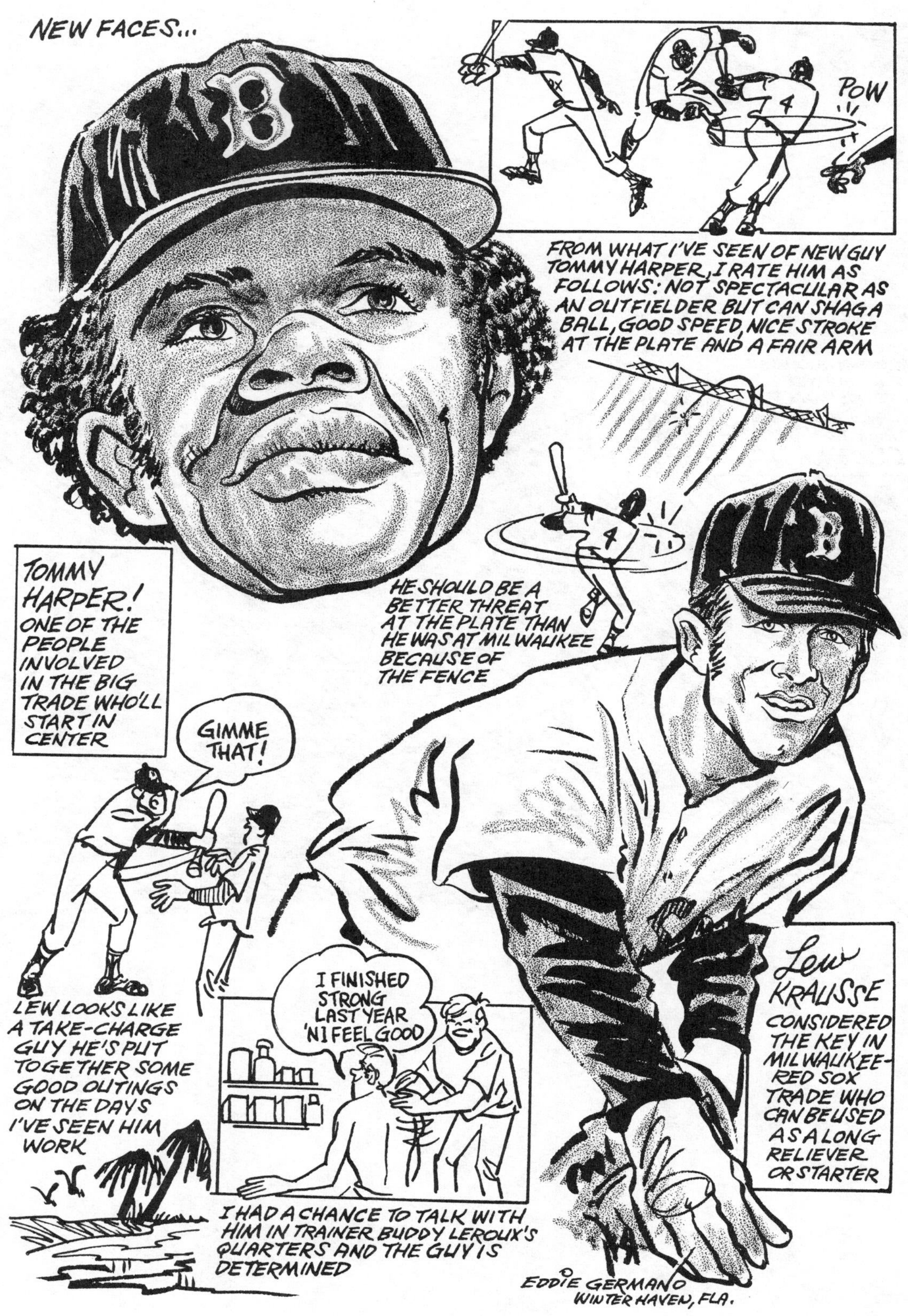
NEW FACES...
POW
FROM WHAT I'VE SEEN OF NEW GUY TOMMY HARPER, I RATE HIM AS FOLLOWS: NOT SPECTACULAR AS AN OUTFIELDER BUT CAN SHAG A BALL, GOOD SPEED, NICE STROKE AT THE PLATE AND A FAIR ARM
TOMMY HARPER! ONE OF THE PEOPLE INVOLVED IN THE BIG TRADE WHO'LL START IN CENTER
HE SHOULD BE A BETTER THREAT AT THE PLATE THAN HE WAS AT MILWAUKEE BECAUSE OF THE FENCE
GIMME THAT!
LEW LOOKS LIKE A TAKE-CHARGE GUY HE'S PUT TOGETHER SOME GOOD OUTINGS ON THE DAYS I'VE SEEN HIM WORK
I FINISHED STRONG LAST YEAR 'N I FEEL GOOD
I HAD A CHANCE TO TALK WITH HIM IN TRAINER BUDDY LEROUX'S QUARTERS AND THE GUY IS DETERMINED
Lew KRAUSSE
CONSIDERED THE KEY IN MILWAUKEE-RED SOX TRADE WHO CAN BE USED AS A LONG RELIEVER OR STARTER
EDDIE GERMANO
WINTER HAVEN, FLA.

DEPTHS OF DESPAIR
THIS SITUATION IS NO LONGER FUNNY !!
BOSTON RED SOX... A.L. EAST CELLAR-DWELLERS
EDDIE GERMANO
PATTIN, MARTY THAT IS, IS RUMBLING ALONG ON A FIVE GAME WIN STREAK... AFTER A BAD START, HE'S NOW SEVEN AND EIGHT...
WINS
OPPOSITION
...THE WAY HE'S GOING THE RED SOX FIGURE TO WIN MORE BATTLES AND MAYBE EVEN THE EASTERN DIV. WAR
EDDIE GERMANO
ENTERPRISE SPORTS

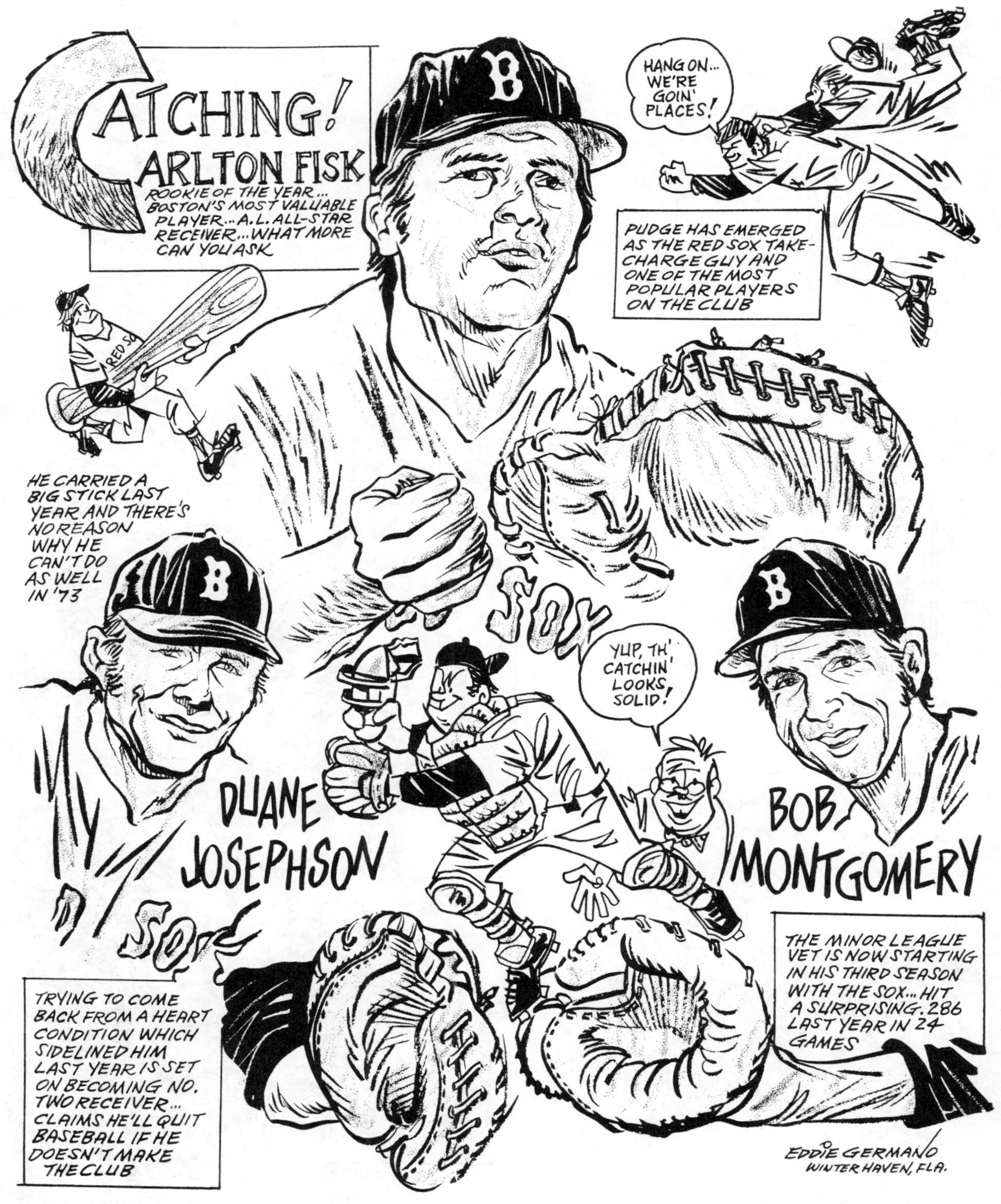
CATCHING!
CARLTON FISK
ROOKIE OF THE YEAR... BOSTON'S MOST VALUABLE PLAYER... A.L. ALL-STAR RECEIVER... WHAT MORE CAN YOU ASK
HANG ON... WE'RE GOIN' PLACES!
PUDGE HAS EMERGED AS THE RED SOX TAKE-CHARGE GUY AND ONE OF THE MOST POPULAR PLAYERS ON THE CLUB
HE CARRIED A BIG STICK LAST YEAR AND THERE'S NO REASON WHY HE CAN'T DO AS WELL IN '73
SOX
YUP, TH' CATCHIN' LOOKS SOLID!
DUANE JOSEPHSON
BOB MONTGOMERY
SOX
THE MINOR LEAGUE VET IS NOW STARTING IN HIS THIRD SEASON WITH THE SOX... HIT A SURPRISING .286 LAST YEAR IN 24 GAMES
TRYING TO COME BACK FROM A HEART CONDITION WHICH SIDELINED HIM LAST YEAR IS SET ON BECOMING NO. TWO RECEIVER... CLAIMS HE'LL QUIT BASEBALL IF HE DOESN'T MAKE THE CLUB
EDDIE GERMANO
WINTER HAVEN, FLA.

I'LL GIVE YA LONBORG, BRETT, LAHOUD, BILLY C. 'N SCOTT FER HARPER, PATTIN, KRAUSSE 'N YAZ!
GULP!
GM FRANK LANE
GM DICK O'CONNELL
ANAHEIM
OAKLAND
MILWAUKEE
EDDIE GERMANO

1973

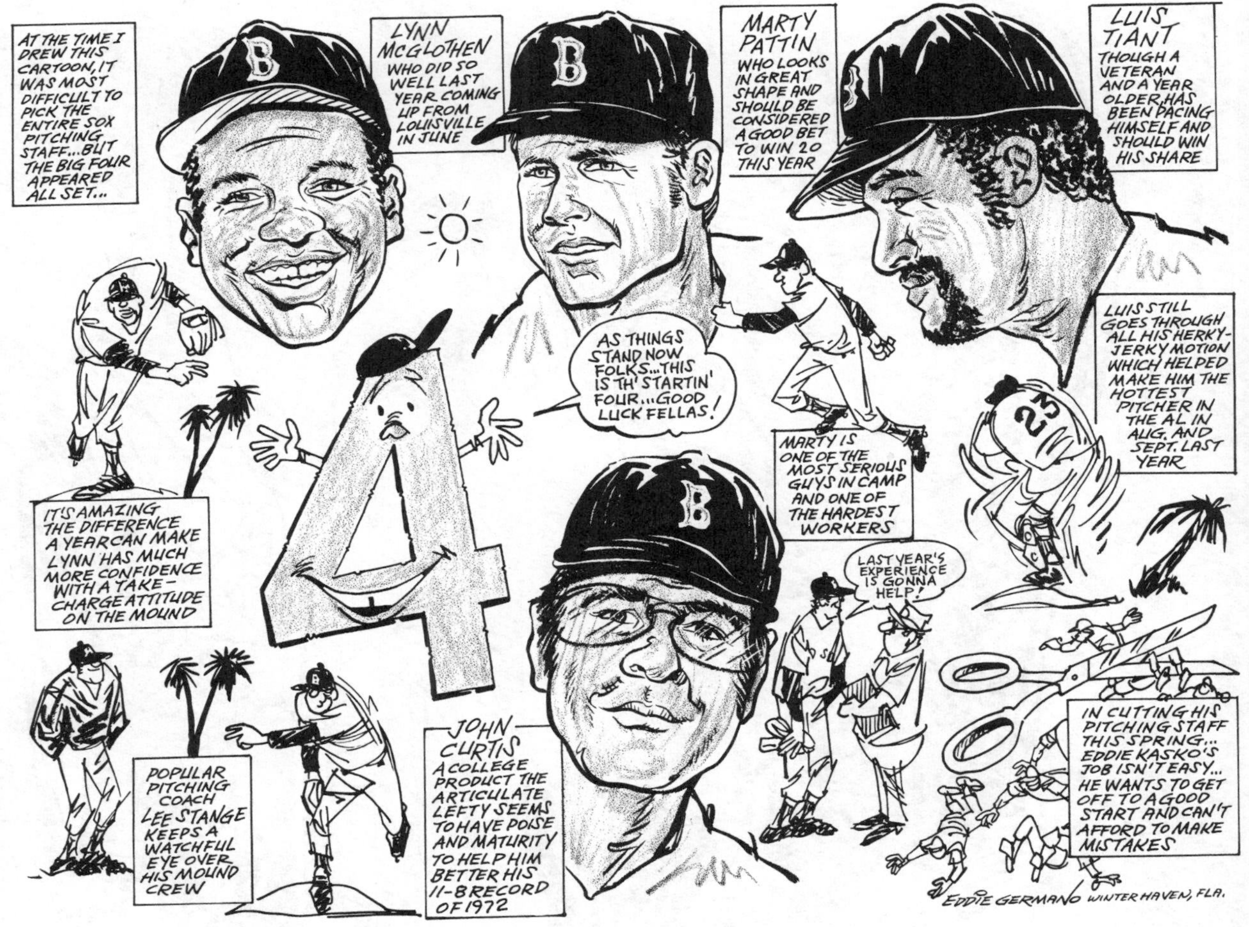

AT THE TIME I DREW THIS CARTOON, IT WAS MOST DIFFICULT TO PICK THE ENTIRE SOX PITCHING STAFF...BUT THE BIG FOUR APPEARED ALL SET...
LYNN McGLOTHEN WHO DID SO WELL LAST YEAR COMING UP FROM LOUISVILLE IN JUNE
MARTY PATTIN WHO LOOKS IN GREAT SHAPE AND SHOULD BE CONSIDERED A GOOD BET TO WIN 20 THIS YEAR
LUIS TIANT THOUGH A VETERAN AND A YEAR OLDER, HAS BEEN PACING HIMSELF AND SHOULD WIN HIS SHARE
AS THINGS STAND NOW FOLKS...THIS IS TH' STARTIN' FOUR...GOOD LUCK FELLAS!
LUIS STILL GOES THROUGH ALL HIS HERKY-JERKY MOTION WHICH HELPED MAKE HIM THE HOTTEST PITCHER IN THE AL IN AUG. AND SEPT. LAST YEAR
MARTY IS ONE OF THE MOST SERIOUS GUYS IN CAMP AND ONE OF THE HARDEST WORKERS
IT'S AMAZING THE DIFFERENCE A YEAR CAN MAKE LYNN HAS MUCH MORE CONFIDENCE WITH A TAKE-CHARGE ATTITUDE ON THE MOUND
LAST YEAR'S EXPERIENCE IS GONNA HELP!
IN CUTTING HIS PITCHING STAFF THIS SPRING... EDDIE KASKO'S JOB ISN'T EASY... HE WANTS TO GET OFF TO A GOOD START AND CAN'T AFFORD TO MAKE MISTAKES
POPULAR PITCHING COACH LEE STANGE KEEPS A WATCHFUL EYE OVER HIS MOUND CREW
JOHN CURTIS A COLLEGE PRODUCT THE ARTICULATE LEFTY SEEMS TO HAVE POISE AND MATURITY TO HELP HIM BETTER HIS 11-8 RECORD OF 1972
EDDIE GERMANO WINTER HAVEN, FLA.

WHO'S BROOKS ROBINSON ?
RED SOX
HIS HITTING BOGGED DOWN LAST YEAR BUT HE FOUND HIMSELF AS A DEFENSIVE THIRD BASEMAN MAKING SOME TOP PLAYS IN THE FIELD DURING THE AUG. AND SEPT. STRETCH DRIVE
TH'HECK WITH IT, SHOW ME AN ITALIAN WHO DOESN'T LIKE T'EAT 'N I'LL SHOW YOU AN UN-HAPPY MAN!
RED SOX
PETRO'S OFF HIS DIET KICK THIS SPRING HOPING TO INCREASE HIS POWER WITH THE BAT
RICO!
PETROCELLI
WINTER HAVEN PROFILES
A.L. PRES. JOE CRONIN...
RED SOX GEN. MGR. DICK O'CONNELL... HOW THEY LOVE THOSE CIGARS!
HE'S ANOTHER CONFIDENT SOX VET WHO FEELS TH'CLUB CAN GO ALL TH' WAY!
EDDIE GERMANO WINTER HAVEN, FLA.

OPENING DAY IS JUST ONE WEEK FROM TODAY AND WITH THIS IN MIND... EDDIE KASKO IS IN THE PROCESS OF MAKING HIS FINAL CUT!
SORRY... BUT IF I DON'T WIN... SOMEDAY IT'LL BE MY HEAD TOO!
WILL YA RECONSIDER IF I PROMISE TO PLAY MY HEAD OFF... OOPS WHAT DID I SAY!
I CAN'T BEAR T'LOOK!
PHIL PHAN
EDDIE GERMANO WINTER HAVEN, FLA.

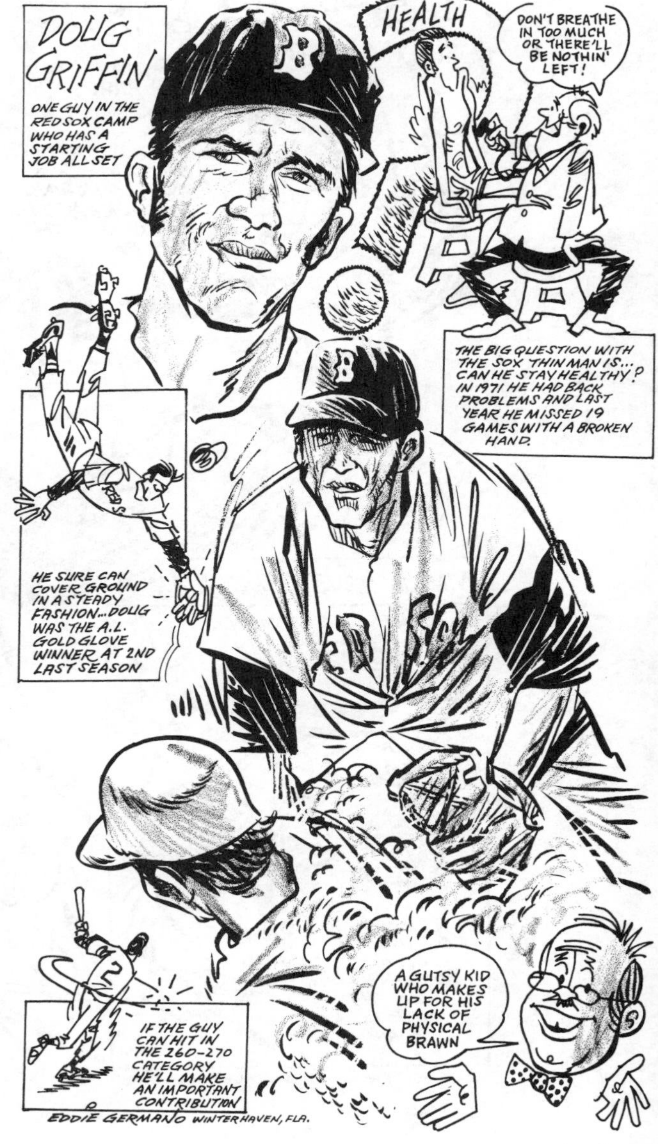
DOUG GRIFFIN
ONE GUY IN THE RED SOX CAMP WHO HAS A STARTING JOB ALL SET
HEALTH
DON'T BREATHE IN TOO MUCH OR THERE'LL BE NOTHIN' LEFT!
THE BIG QUESTION WITH THE SOX THIN MAN IS... CAN HE STAY HEALTHY? IN 1971 HE HAD BACK PROBLEMS AND LAST YEAR HE MISSED 19 GAMES WITH A BROKEN HAND.
HE SURE CAN COVER GROUND IN A STEADY FASHION... DOUG WAS THE A.L. GOLD GLOVE WINNER AT 2ND LAST SEASON
IF THE GUY CAN HIT IN THE 260-270 CATEGORY HE'LL MAKE AN IMPORTANT CONTRIBUTION
A GUTSY KID WHO MAKES UP FOR HIS LACK OF PHYSICAL BRAWN
EDDIE GERMANO WINTER HAVEN, FLA.

NEW ARRIVALS
GARMAN
CURTIS
FISK
COOPER
BENIQUEZ
OGLIVIE
MILLER
LINEUP
EDDIE KASKO
EDDIE GERMANO

REGARDLESS OF WHERE THE RED SOX FINISH, NO ONE EVER DREAMED THAT ORLANDO CEPEDA WOULD COME THROUGH THE WAY HE HAS ON THOSE SCARRED KNEES OF HIS
AMAZIN' HOW THOSE LEGS HAVE PRODUCED SUCH (FEETS!)
EDDIE GERMANO

1974

FENWAY PARK'S REVOLVING DOOR
WILL YA LOVE ME A YEAR FROM NOW ?
EDDIE K.
NEW SKIPPER DARRELL JOHNSON
DARRELL BABY! I'VE BEEN EXPECTIN' YOU!
PHIL PHAN
EDDIE GERMANO

LET'S TAKE A PEEK BEHIND THE SCENES WITH NEW MANAGER
DARRELL JOHNSON
ONE OF THE THINGS HE WILL DO IS CALL A PLAYER TO ONE SIDE AND HAVE A PRIVATE CHAT...STRICTLY HUSH-HUSH
22
RED SOX
IT MAY NOT HELP HIM WIN GAMES BUT THAT PROFILE IS STRICTLY HOLLYWOOD... RIGHT GALS?
HIS PRESS CONFERENCES ARE USUALLY ALL BUSINESS BUT A QUICK WIT COMES THROUGH AS WELL
RED SOX
RED SOX
AT TIMES HE WILL PICK OUT A SPOT APART FROM EVERYONE AND PONDER OVER HIS NOTATIONS
"MY JOB RIGHT NOW IS TO GET THESE GUYS READY TO PLAY BALL AND EVERYONE IS GETTING A FAIR CHANCE" DARRELL
WHILE HE DOESN'T APPEAR TOUGH, THERE IS A STERN AUSTERE MANNER ABOUT THE MAN WHICH COMMANDS RESPECT
EDDIE GERMANO WINTER HAVEN, FLA.
HIGH HOPES
THE RED SOX ARE IN THE PROCESS OF EXTENDING THEIR FLAG POLE IN YONDER CENTER FIELD AT FRIENDLY FENWAY...COULD IT BE THEY NEED THE EXTENSION TO ACCOMMODATE THE '74 PENNANT?
PLAYER TRADES
74
EASY UP THERE !
PHIL PHAN
EDDIE GERMANO

LIFE BEGINS AT 40
THE RED SOX HAVE SEVERAL KID SHORTSTOPS DOWN HERE...
GOO!
C'MON! ON YOUR TOES!
THE GUY IS A STUDY IN PERPETUAL MOTION, WHEN NOT TAKING INFIELD OR BATTING PRACTISE, YOU'LL FIND HIM PLAYING PEPPER WITH YAZ AND HIS 2ND BASE COMBO DOUG GRIFFIN
...BUT WHEN THE OPENING GONG SOUNDS, IT'LL BE AGELESS
LUIS APARICIO!
WHO'LL BE STARTING HIS 18th SEASON IN THE BIGGIES AT SHORT
LUIS SI!
RED SOX
PLAYING BALL PRACTICALLY ALL YEAR 'ROUND INCLUDING THE WINTER LEAGUE, HE'S NEVER OUT OF SHAPE AND BARES A STOMACH AS FLAT AS AN IRONING BOARD
ONE THING THAT HAS COME UP HERE ARE HIS 40-YEAR-OLD LEGS... THERE IS INDICATION OF A MINOR PROBLEM IN THIS DEPT.
SPRING TRAINING PROFILES...
SAY H'LO TO ALL MY AREA FRIENDS!
I BUMPED INTO AL FARLEY FORMER MIDDLEBORO HIGH BASKETBALL AND BASEBALL COACH, AL IS NOW RETIRED AND LOOKS TRIM 'N FIT... A REAL BAROMETER OF THE GOOD LIFE IN FLORIDA
EDDIE GERMANO... WINTER HAVEN, FLA.

1975

All season long Sox fans thrilled to the deeds of rookies Fred Lynn and Jim Rice. Both earned over 100 RBIs, and Lynn became Rookie of the Year and MVP. Solid play by the rest of the team helped push the Sox to the top. Then the World Series brought together the Red Sox and the Cincinnati Reds in one of the greatest championships ever played.

CLANG CLANG
WHERE THERE'S SMOKE, THERE'S FIRE BUT NOT FOR LONG!
JIM WILLOUGHBY
HE'S NOT OVER-POWERING LIKE SOME OF THE GREAT RELIEF PITCHERS OF THE PAST BUT HE GETS THE JOB DONE... AND ONE OF THE REAL BIG REASONS WHY THE RED SOX ARE WHERE THEY ARE
EDDIE GERMANO
DESIGNATED STAR
TO BE HONEST, BASED ON WHAT I SAW IN SPRING TRAINING, I WASN'T SURE THAT JIM RICE WAS READY FOR MAJOR LEAGUE PITCHING...
BUT RICE HAS BEEN MIGHTY TASTY AT THE DISH FOR THE RED SOX THUS FAR...
HE HAS FILLED THE DH PICTURE SO WELL, IT'S BEEN TOUGH ON THE COMEBACKING TONY C. TO MAKE A SOLID BID
EDDIE GERMANO

SHILLELAGH AND ALL
'N DIVIL A PITCHER WHO'LL MONKEY WITH ME... WHEN I HAVE IT IN ME HAND!
DENNY DOYLE
WITH THE BOSOX ON THEIR LONG ROAD TRIP AND FIRST PLACE IN THE A.L. EAST AT STAKE, THE BATTLING IRISHMAN HOPES TO CONTINUE TO HANG IN TOUGH
EDDIE GERMANO
NOSTALGIC SPORTS FANS RECALL THOSE GREAT RED SOX YANKEE MEETINGS OF YESTER-YEAR...
NEW YORK
...AND THIS WEEKEND AT FENWAY THOSE OL' RIVALS ARE RELIVING THE PAST AND FIRST PLACE IS AT STAKE TOO... JUST THE WAY IT USED TO BE
EDDIE GERMANO

Diamond in the Rough

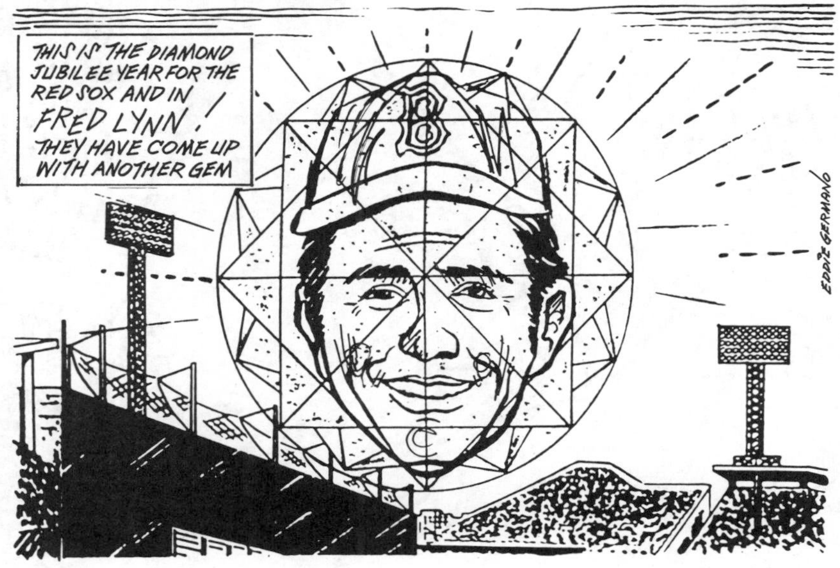

1974 RED SOX NIGHTMARE

IT WAS JUST ABOUT THIS TIME LAST SEASON WHEN THAT 7½ GAME LEAD STARTED TO DISSIPATE... BUT THIS IS ANOTHER YEAR AN OUR OL' BUDDY PHIL PHAN REALLY HAS NOTHING TO FEAR... I KNOW... I'M SURE... I THINK... I HOPE!

EDDIE GERMANO

HE STANDS TALL!

CARLTON FISK! HE CAN DO IT ALL!

RED SOX

EDDIE GERMANO
ENTERPRISE SPORTS

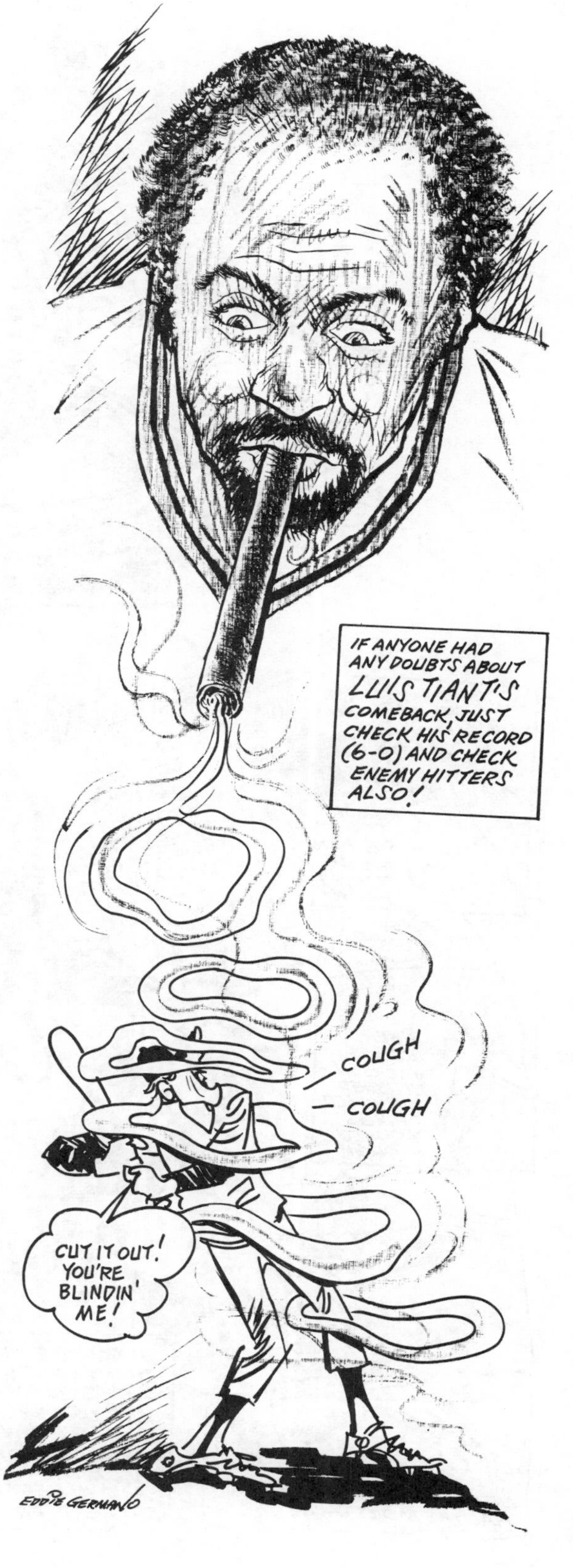

IF ANYONE HAD ANY DOUBTS ABOUT LUIS TIANT'S COMEBACK, JUST CHECK HIS RECORD (6-0) AND CHECK ENEMY HITTERS ALSO!

COUGH

COUGH

CUT IT OUT! YOU'RE BLINDIN' ME!

EDDIE GERMANO

NEAR AND YET SO FAR
RED SOX
1st PLACE A.L. EAST
EDDIE GERMANO
ENTERPRISE SPORTS

L.F. WALL
WOE IS ME!
RUMORS HAVE IT THAT OL' SAL BANDO WANTS TO COME TO FENWAY
OH... OH!
YAZ FOUND THE SCREEN TO GET THE SOX ON THE VICTORY TRAIL
RICO SHATTERED THE LIGHT TOWER WITH HIS HR
WHEN REGGIE JACKSON CLUBBED HIS HOMER, THINGS LOOKED TOUGH
DICK DRAGO CAME UP WITH THE SAVE AND A BIG ONE IT WAS
FRED LYNN COVERED CF LIKE A BLANKET
GOOD BYE CHARLIE...
...SORRY TO SEE YOU GO
CHARLIE FINLEY WAS SERENADED BUT PROVED TO BE A GOOD SPORT
IN 1967, THE FLAG CHANT WOULD SAY "WE'VE GOT YAZ!" AND YESTERDAY WE SURE DID HAVE YAZ... THE OL' PRO DID IT ALL, BOTH ON OFFENSE AND IN LEFT FIELD TO SHATTER THE A'S
1975 AMERICAN LEAGUE CHAMPIONS
NEMESIS ROLLIE FINGERS HAD HIS MOUSTACHE CLIPPED
EDDIE GERMANO at FENWAY PARK
WELL KIDDIES, ONE MORE WIN AND THE FLAG FLIES OVER FENWAY... HONEST!

BOSTON RED SOX
1975 A.L. CHAMPIONS
RED SOX
PHIL and
PHYLLIS
PHAN
EDDIE GERMANO

And the Beat Goes On!

IN WHAT MAY HAVE BEEN THE GREATEST BASE-BALL GAME EVER PLAYED AT FENWAY, THE RED SOX DIS-MANTLED THE RED MACHINE LAST NIGHT TO SEND THE 1975 WORLD SERIES INTO TONIGHT'S 7th AND DECIDING GAME
PUDGE FISK'S WINNING HOMER IN THE 12th
THE BIG RED MACHINE
LYNN'S THREE-RUN HR
EVANS' GREAT CATCH
BERNIE CARBO'S THREE-RUN HOMER TO TIE IT IN THE 8th
FINE RELIEF PITCHING BY MORET, DRAGO AND WISE
MY POOR HEART... IT CAN'T TAKE ANY MORE!
PHIL PHAN
EDDIE GERMANO

1
A FULL MOON FOR SPACE-MAN!
YER OL' PAL PHIL PHAN WAS AT FENWAY PARK LAST NIGHT TO ROOT THE RED SOX HOME
2
BANG!
WHEN CARBO LED OFF WITH HIS DOUBLE, ALL WAS BRIGHT
3
RED SOX
THEN IN THE 3RD THE HOME HEROES SCORED THREE BIGONES
4
TWO-RUN HR
BUT PEREZ BLASTED A LOLLIPOP BILL LEE PITCH INTO KENMORE SQUARE
5
PETE ROSE A THORN IN THE RED SOX SIDE TIED IT UP 3-3, IN THE 7th
6
MUST BE HERE SUMPLACE!
IN THE 9th SOX CHUCKERS COULDN'T FIND THE PLATE
7
AND JOE MORGAN'S SINGLE TO CENTER GAVE THE REDS A 4-3 LEAD
8
YAZ FLIED OUT FOR THE FINAL OUT OF THE '75 SEASON AND IT WAS ALL OVER
9
BOSTON RED SOX A.L. CHAMPIONS 1975
WE DIDN'T WIN TH' WORLD SERIES BUT WE STILL HAVE TH' PENNANT
10
AND WHAT A THRILLIN' YEAR IT WAS!
11
BUT YA KNOW SUMPIN'?
12
I THINK I'M GONNA CRY MY HEART OUT!
EDDIE GERMANO

1976-1980

The late seventies were a roller-coaster ride for the Sox. Under manager Don Zimmer, the team ran hot and cold. A long slide started when they blew their big 1978 lead and lost the terrible tiebreaker to the Yankees. At the same time, front-office troubles began generating more headlines than play on the field.

BEFORE THE SEASON, I WAS ONE OF THOSE WHO INDICATED THAT CARL YASTRZEMSKI SHOULD BE RESTED MORE THIS YEAR...

BASEBALL FOUNTAIN OF YOUTH

...BUT THE WAY THE 37 YEAR OLD YAZ IS PLAYING THESE DAYS HE COULD GO ON FOREVER

GLUB GLUB

DRINK ON... DRINK ON!

PHIL PHAN

EDDIE GERMANO

1 LET'S FOLLOW OUR OL' PAL PHIL PHAN ALONG AND SEE WHAT HE HAS DISCOVERED ABOUT THE 1976 EDITION OF THE RED SOX...
WITH OR WITHOUT TH' RUG... IT'S TH' SAME OL' LOOIE!
2 FIRST HE SEES A SOLID STARTING ROTATION PLUS SOME GOOD RELIEF MEN AND SPOT STARTERS...
BILL LEE
FERGUSON JENKINS
RICK WISE
LUIS TIANT
PLUS CLEVELAND... WILLOUGHBY and HOUSE
PLUS CARBO 'N MILLER!
3 NEXT, LOOKING OVER THE OUTFIELD, IT APPEARS TO BE THE STRONGEST PART OF THE CLUB LED BY FRED LYNN JIM RICE and DWIGHT EVANS...
4 LED BY CAPT. CARL AT FIRST, THE INFIELD LOOKS FORMIDABLE BARRING INJURIES OR SICKNESS...
PUFF, PUFF YAZ IS SURE IN BETTER SHAPE THEN I AM!
YAZ
DOYLE
BURLESON
RICO
GRIFFIN
and the SURPRISING...
...DILLARD
5 THE CATCHING IS IN THE CAPABLE HANDS OF PUDGE FISK WITH BACKUP BY ANY OF THESE GUYS... MONTGOMERY, MERCHANT OR BLACKWELL...
6 THE D-H DEPT. LOOKS POTENT TOO WITH COOPER JOHNSON CARBO AND MAYBE EVEN BALAZ A POSSIBILITY
D-H
IN FACT, THINGS LOOK SO GOOD... I CAN'T BEAR T'LOOK ANYMORE FOR FEAR IT'S ONLY A DREAM!
EDDIE GERMANO

ONE OF THE MAJOR REASONS WHY THE RED SOX HAVEN'T BEEN ABLE TO MOVE UP IN THE A.L. EAST IS THE LARGE AMOUNT LEFT **STRANDED**

HELP!
HELP!
HELP!
HELP!
HELP!

I'M COMIN'
I'M COMIN'
I'M HOPIN'
!

HITTING

EDDIE GERMANO
ENTERPRISE SPORTS

1977

I WAS JUST WONDERING WHAT MIGHT HAPPEN IF THE RED SOX ALLOWED WOMEN REPORTERS IN THEIR CLUBHOUSE
EETS CALIFORNIA YELLOW... YOU EEZ NOW A BLOND
LUIS TIANT WOULD SHOW SAMPLES OF HIS FAVORITE PAINT
UGH
JUST A PINCH BETWEEN YOUR TEETH 'N GUMS
PUDGE FISK MIGHT INSIST ON THE GALS GIVING HIS CHAW TOBACCO A TRY
WAIT'LL THE GIRLS FIND OUT WHERE BILL LEE HOLDS HIS INTERVIEWS
YOU'RE NOT TALKIN' T'MY HUSBAND!
SOME WIVES WILL HAVE CENSORSHIP CODES I'M SURE
YOU MR. ZIMMER?
WHO TH' HELL DIDJA EXPECT... ROBERT REDFORD?
THE GALS WILL FIND THE SOX SKIPPER A CANDID FELLOW
HOW ABOUT TOWELING MY BACK, HONEY
THE LADIES MAY HAVE TO PITCH IN WITH POST-SHOWER CHORES
EDDIE GERMANO
WHAT IF NEWSMEN GET TO GO INTO GIRL ATHLETES LOCKER ROOMS
IMAGINE INTERVIEWIN' BILLY-JEAN KING!
YE CARTOON-IST

I'VE ALWAYS LIKED BALL-PLAYERS WHO PLAY TOUGH...
GRR
...THERE AREN'T THAT MANY THESE DAYS WHO'VE GOT THE BULLDOG IN 'EM EXCEPT A FEW...
SO WHAT'S A BRICK WALL!
...AND ONE WHO FITS THE HARD-NOSE IMAGE IS
BUTCH HOBSON
THE RED SOX HARD-PLAYING THIRD SACKER
EDDIE GERMANO

SPRING FEVER...
THIS IS A TOUGHIE... DO I CARRY NINE PITCHERS OR ELEVEN ?
DON ZIMMER HAS SOME IMPORTANT DECISIONS AS THE SEASON DRAWS NEAR DAY-BY-DAY
NOW THIS IS HOW I DID IT
TED WILLIAMS HAS BEEN THE CENTER OF ATTRACTION EVERYWHERE
YA...BUT I'M NO TED WILLIAMS
RICK WISE'S PITCHING HASN'T MADE IT ANY EASIER FOR THE SOX TO GET RID OF HIM
DENNY DOYLE, A DISCONSOLATE FIGURE KNOWING TIME IS RUNNING OUT FOR HIM
JERRY REMY'S THREAT ON THE BASES IS A FAR CRY FROM THE PLODDERS OF OTHER SOX CLUBS
IT'S MAH HITTIN' THAT COUNTS!
REPORTS ON GEORGE SCOTT'S GIRTH AREN'T ENCOURAGING
A BIG QUESTION TO BE ANSWERED IS HOW SOUND WILL FRED LYNN AND DWIGHT EVANS BE FROM THEIR INJURIES...IF OK... THEY HELP MAKE UP ONE OF THE BEST OUTFIELDS IN BASEBALL ALONG WITH YAZ
HMM... ECKERSLY, ECKERSLY, ECKERSLY...
LAKE LU-LU
WITH TRADE RUMORS RAMPANT, NEW SOX GENERAL MANAGER HAYWOOD SULLIVAN HAS EVEN MORE OPPORTUNITY TO GET HIS FEET WET IN THE PLAYER-SWAPPING DEPT.
YAWKEY WAY
TICKET OFFICE
I WAS IN THE VICINITY OF FENWAY PARK AND WAS AMAZED AT THE LINES OF FANS LOOKING TO BUY TICKETS, GETTING DUCATS FOR BIG GAMES ISN'T GOING TO BE EASY HONEY!
EDDIE GERMANO

OUT OF THIS WORLD
BILL LEE OFTEN TIMES REFERRED TO AS THE MOONMAN AND SPACE-MAN BE-CAUSE OF HIS FAR-OUT LIFE STYLE...
LEE'S SPACELAB
...FINDS HIMSELF SITTING PRETTY WITH A 7-2 RECORD AND A 1.92 ERA... IMAGINE, THE HOSE WANTED TO TRADE HIM OFF EARLIER THIS YEAR
LONG AS YOU KEEP WINNIN' US MERE MORTALS WON'T MIND!
EDDIE GERMANO SPORTS

WISE AS AN OWL
IT WAS NO SECRET THAT RICK WISE WANTED OUT AND THE RED SOX WERE ALL SET TO ACCOMMODATE HIM...
YOU'VE PUT ME OUT ON A LIMB... HOW CAN I TRADE YOU NOW?
RED SOX
...SO WHAT HAPPENS... THE WISE OL' OWL HAS GONE OUT AND PITCHED SOME GREAT BALL THIS SPRING FORCING SOX BRASS TO CHANGE THEIR PLANS TO GET RID OF HIM
EDDIE GERMANO

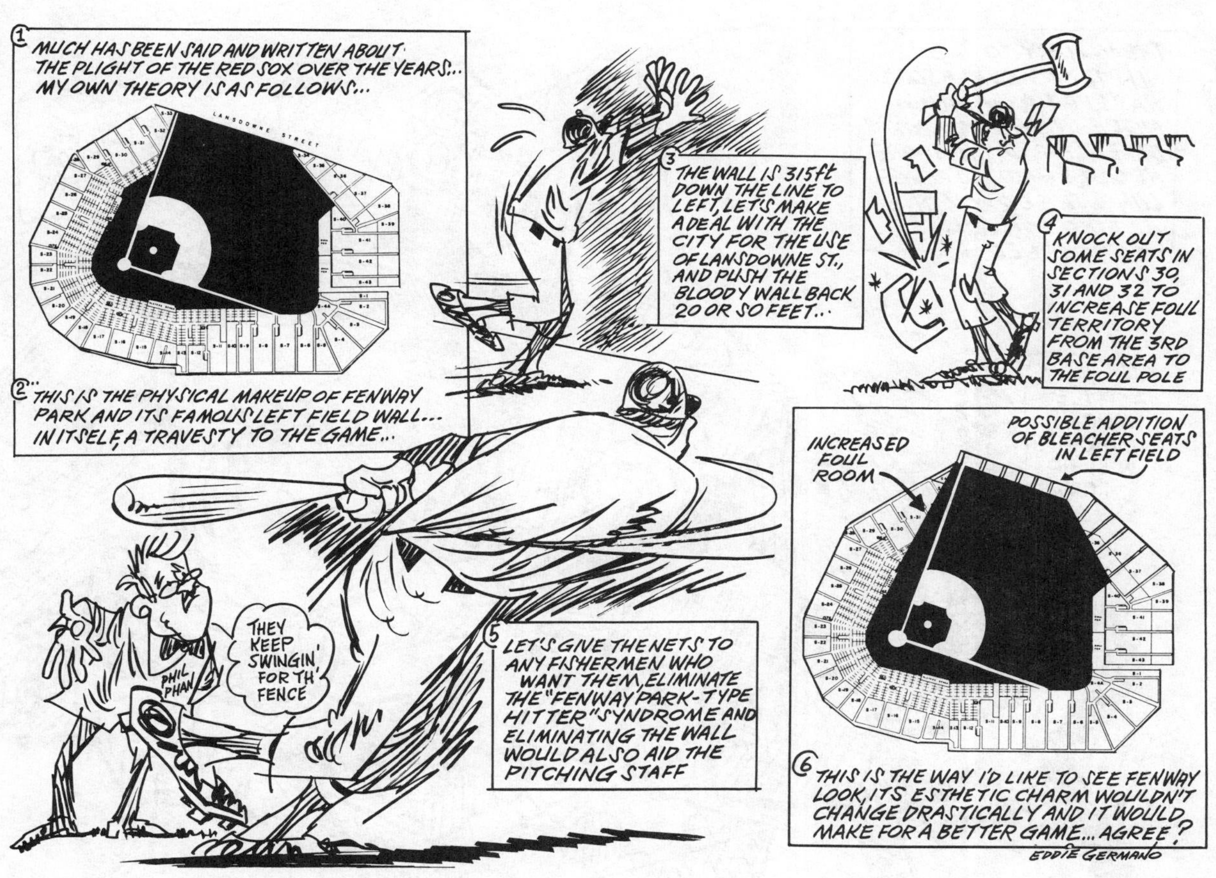

1 MUCH HAS BEEN SAID AND WRITTEN ABOUT THE PLIGHT OF THE RED SOX OVER THE YEARS... MY OWN THEORY IS AS FOLLOWS...
LANSDOWNE STREET
2 ...THIS IS THE PHYSICAL MAKEUP OF FENWAY PARK AND ITS FAMOUS LEFT FIELD WALL... IN ITSELF, A TRAVESTY TO THE GAME...
3 THE WALL IS 315ft DOWN THE LINE TO LEFT, LET'S MAKE A DEAL WITH THE CITY FOR THE USE OF LANSDOWNE ST., AND PUSH THE BLOODY WALL BACK 20 OR SO FEET...
4 KNOCK OUT SOME SEATS IN SECTIONS 30, 31 AND 32 TO INCREASE FOUL TERRITORY FROM THE 3RD BASE AREA TO THE FOUL POLE
THEY KEEP SWINGIN' FOR TH' FENCE
PHIL PHAN
5 LET'S GIVE THE NETS TO ANY FISHERMEN WHO WANT THEM, ELIMINATE THE "FENWAY PARK-TYPE HITTER" SYNDROME AND ELIMINATING THE WALL WOULD ALSO AID THE PITCHING STAFF
INCREASED FOUL ROOM
POSSIBLE ADDITION OF BLEACHER SEATS IN LEFT FIELD
6 THIS IS THE WAY I'D LIKE TO SEE FENWAY LOOK, ITS ESTHETIC CHARM WOULDN'T CHANGE DRASTICALLY AND IT WOULD MAKE FOR A BETTER GAME... AGREE?
EDDIE GERMANO

1978

THE INJURY TO THE HUSTLING BURLESON HAS LEFT A GAPING HOLE IN THE RED SOX DEFENSE AND THE SOONER HE GETS BACK TO PLUG-GING THE CRACK THE BETTER FOR ALL CONCERNED
SHORTSTOP
WE'RE ALMOST READY
A LITTLE MORE MORTAR WILL DO IT!
RED SOX
RICK BURLESON CONTRACTING CO.
EDDIE GERMANO

I TOOK A WALK OVER TO THE RED SOX MINOR LEAGUE COMPLEX TO SEE THE LAST OF THE .400 HITTERS...
TED WILLIAMS...
TED'S INSTRUCTING RAW KIDS WHO CHEW TOBACCO BUT AS YET ARE BARELY SHAVING...
THE BIG GUY STILL CUTS AN IMPOSING FIGURE DESPITE AN AMPLE PAUNCH...
TED INSTRUCTS HIS STUDENTS TO GET HIP-ACTION INTO THE PITCH FOR ADDED POWER...
TURN TH' CLOCK BACK 30 YEARS
AH... NOSTALGIA
A HUGE GALLERY OF FANS PEER THROUGH THE FENCE TO GET A PEEK AT THE GREAT HITTER IN ACTION
EDDIE GERMANO
WINTER HAVEN, FLA.
STRETCH DRIVE
HOPE ONE OFF-SETS THE OTHER
PITCHING & TIMELY HITTING
RED SOX
1st PLACE
POOR DEFENSE UP THE MIDDLE
EDDIE GERMANO

THAT WAS A TON OF MONEY THE RED SOX DISHED OUT TO GET MIKE TORREZ...
TO MIKE... WITH LOVE
WAIT'LL THEY GET A LOAD OF THIS GUY
RED SOX
GUESS THEY MEAN BUSINESS
RED SOX
EDDIE GERMANO
...BUT WHAT THE SOX HAVE RECEIVED IN RETURN FOR THEIR HUGE INVESTMENT ISN'T EXACTLY WHAT THEY BARGAINED FOR

CAMPBELL'S OUT OF THE SOUP

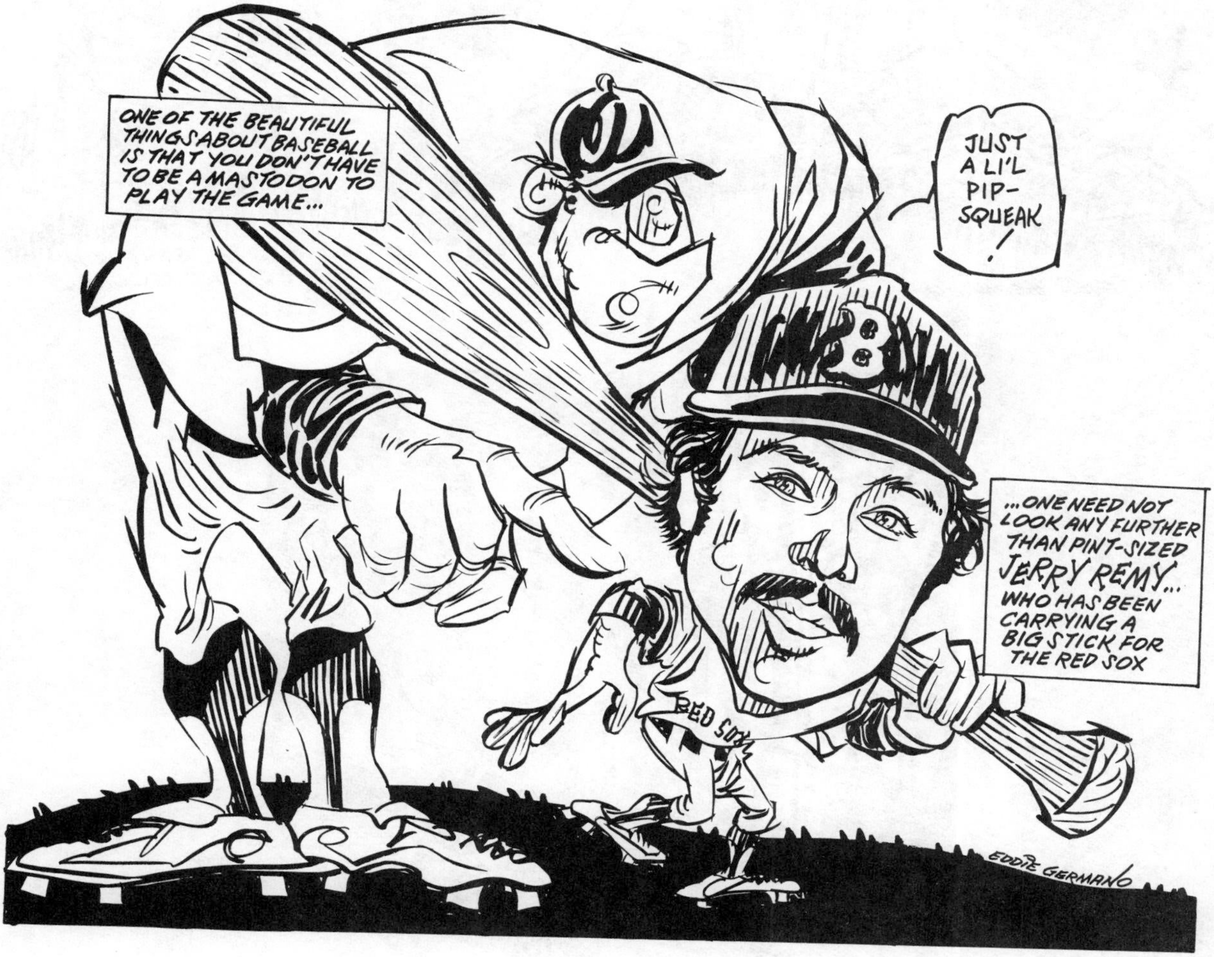

ONE OF THE BEAUTIFUL THINGS ABOUT BASEBALL IS THAT YOU DON'T HAVE TO BE A MASTODON TO PLAY THE GAME...

JUST A LI'L PIP-SQUEAK!

...ONE NEED NOT LOOK ANY FURTHER THAN PINT-SIZED JERRY REMY... WHO HAS BEEN CARRYING A BIG STICK FOR THE RED SOX

RED SOX

EDDIE GERMANO

IN ADDITION TO THE PROBLEM OF CATCHING THE ORIOLES... THE RED SOX ARE ALSO CONCERNED ABOUT YAZ'S ACHING DOGS...

TALK ABOUT PLAYING IN PAIN

DID YOU HEAR BARKING ?

BOW WOW

GRR

...GOING INTO THE STRETCH DRIVE, THE OL' PRO IS SORELY NEEDED

EDDIE GERMANO

DESPITE YESTERDAY'S VICTORY, PENNANT HOPES FOR THE RED SOX ARE STILL PRECARIOUS AS THE SEASON WINDS DOWN...
WHATEVER HAPPENED TO MY BIG LEAD ?
RED SOX
... AND THE GUY ONE HAS TO FEEL SORRY FOR IS OL' PRO CARL YASTRZEMSKI... HE WANTS A PENNANT AND SERIES VICTORY SO BAD HE CAN TASTE IT
NOBODY'S HUSTLED HARDER THAN TH' CAPTAIN
JUST 13 GAMES TO GO
EDDIE GERMANO

THERE IS NOTHING LIKE THE THRILL OF ANTICIPATION PRIOR TO A YANKEES-RED SOX GAME...
...BUT LAST NIGHT WAS NO CONTEST AS THE BOYS FROM THE BRONX SHELLED MIKE TORREZ
WHAT TH' HELL'S GOIN' ON?
BEFORE FANS SETTLED IN THEIR SEATS, IT WAS 5-0
PUDGE FISK GAVE THE HOME FOLKS SOMETHING TO CHEER ABOUT
BOB MONTGOMERY FINALLY GOT INTO A GAME...BENCH SPLINTERS AND ALL
2 MORE ERRORS!
YA GOTTA FEEL SORRY FOR BUTCH HOBSON
POW
A DRAGO FAST BALL BEANED THURMAN MUNSON
HI! IT'S ME !!!
BUZZZZZZ
STOP BREATHIN' ON ME!
THE YANKEES ARE FAR FROM DEAD AND ARE NOW JUST THREE OUT...
...BUT BEFORE WE PUSH THE PANIC BUTTON KIDDIES, TONIGHT'S ANOTHER NIGHT...HANG IN THERE!!!
EDDIE GERMANO at Fenway Park

THE BITTER END
THINGS LOOKED GOOD FOR MIKE TORREZ AND THE RED SOX IN THE EARLY GOING YESTERDAY
RED SOX
NEW
AW GEE!
BUCKY DENT JUST MADE THE SCREEN WITH HIS SHOT TO PUT N.Y. IN THE LEAD
44
CAPTAIN YAZ CLOCKED ONE TO GIVE THE SOX THE LEAD IN THE SECOND
REMY MADE A FINE PLAY ON CHAMBLISS TO HELP THE CAUSE
WHAT PROVED TO BE THE BACK BREAKER WAS THE BLAST BY REGGIE JACKSON WHICH PROVED TO BE THE WINNING RUN AND FURTHER PROVED THAT REGGIE IS A MONEY PLAYER

THE RED SOX DIDN'T LOSE AT THE GATE... 2,320,643 PASSED THROUGH FENWAY TURNSTYLES FOR A NEW ATTENDANCE RECORD IN '78
I'M SICK OF WAITIN' 'TILL NEXT YEAR!
15
GEORGE SCOTT'S K WITH TWO ON HURT
RED SOX FANS MAY BE RIGHT
YAZ POPPED UP TO END THE GAME AND LATER IN THE CLUB-HOUSE, IT WAS A SORRY THING TO SEE THE OL' PRO CRY
PINIELLA'S STAB ON LYNN SAVED TWO RUNS AND MAYBE THE GAME
EDDIE GERMANO at FENWAY PARK

1979

TO SAY THAT DON ZIMMER IS SITTING ON A POWDER KEG, IS TELLING IT LIKE IT IS...
I'M SURE YOU REALIZE MY PREDICAMENT... SO LET'S GO GET 'EM!
THURS. OPENER
GOTCHA SKIP!
...IT'S IMPERATIVE THAT THE SOX GET OFF TO A GOOD START OR THE NATIVES WILL BE A RESTLESS LOT
EDDIE GERMANO

ON FIRE
PENNANT
FOLLOW ME!
BACK IN 1975 FRED DID IT ALL AS HE LED THE RED SOX TO THE PENNANT AND CHOSEN MVP OF THE A.L.
.318 AVE.
24 HOMERS
73 RBI'S
SOMEBODY, GET A HOSE!
FRED LYNN
THIS YEAR HE'S ON ANOTHER HOT STREAK, SCORCHING OPPOSING PITCHERS WITH HIS FLAMING BAT WHILE PLAYING A SOLID C F
EDDIE GERMANO

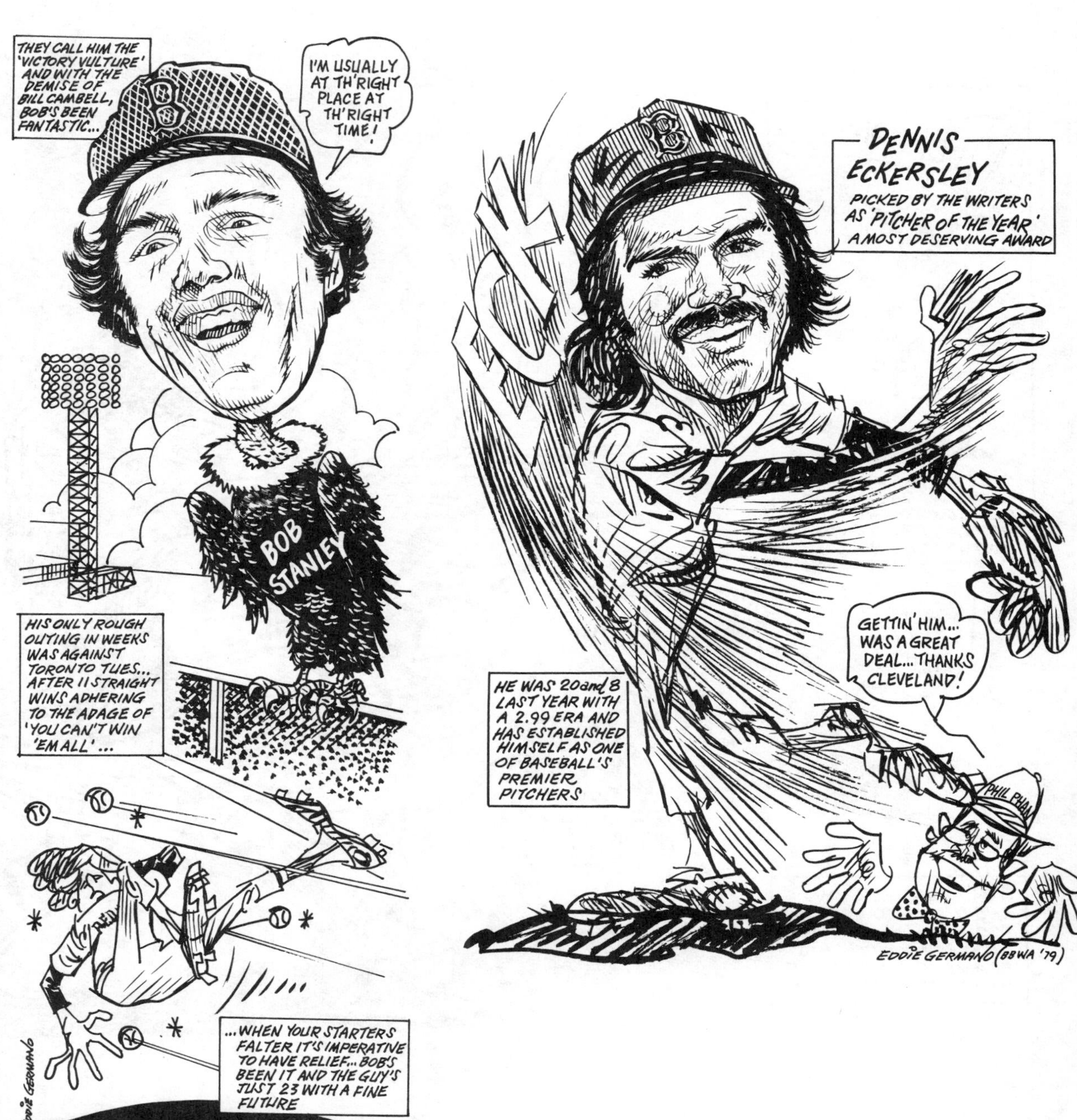
THEY CALL HIM THE 'VICTORY VULTURE' AND WITH THE DEMISE OF BILL CAMBELL, BOB'S BEEN FANTASTIC...
I'M USUALLY AT TH'RIGHT PLACE AT TH'RIGHT TIME!
BOB STANLEY
HIS ONLY ROUGH OUTING IN WEEKS WAS AGAINST TORONTO TUES... AFTER 11 STRAIGHT WINS ADHERING TO THE ADAGE OF 'YOU CAN'T WIN 'EM ALL'...
...WHEN YOUR STARTERS FALTER IT'S IMPERATIVE TO HAVE RELIEF... BOB'S BEEN IT AND THE GUY'S JUST 23 WITH A FINE FUTURE
EDDIE GERMANO
DENNIS ECKERSLEY
PICKED BY THE WRITERS AS 'PITCHER OF THE YEAR' A MOST DESERVING AWARD
ECK
HE WAS 20 and 8 LAST YEAR WITH A 2.99 ERA AND HAS ESTABLISHED HIMSELF AS ONE OF BASEBALL'S PREMIER PITCHERS
GETTIN' HIM... WAS A GREAT DEAL... THANKS CLEVELAND!
PHIL PHAN
EDDIE GERMANO (BBWA '79)

SAME OLD LINE
C'MON YOU CAN DO IT!!! C'MON!
OVER .500 MARK
IT'S MOST DISCOURAGING TO SEE OUR FENWAY HEROS STRANDED NEAR THE .500 MARK FOR MOST OF THE SEASON...
EEEK!
YIPES!
SOX
OOPS!
JUST WHEN THEY APPEAR TO MAKE A MOVE THE CLUB BACKS OFF...CAN IT BE THAT AT BEST THIS IS A .500 BALL TEAM?
EDDIE GERMANO
ENTERPRISE SPORTS
A CLOSED BOOK
THE RED SOX CLOSED THEIR 1979 HOME SEASON LAST NIGHT AND OUR OL' BUDDY PHIL PHAN MUST WAIT FOR ANOTHER YEAR TO REALIZE HIS DREAM (MAYBE)
PENNANT
SAME OLD STORY
RED SOX... '79
EDDIE GERMANO

1980

LID LIFTER
@☆%!
BIGGEST CHEER "ZIM" EVER GOT WHEN HE WAS GIVEN THE GATE BY UMP SPRINGSTEAD
AT LONG LAST!
RICHIE HEBNER FINALLY MADE IT TO FENWAY
HONOR OF FIRST FENWAY HOMER OF THE YEAR GOES TO FRED LYNN
HARDY FANS, SITTING THROUGH THE COLD 'N RAIN
JES FOLLOW ME!
HONK
HONK
'N AWAY WE GO!
NOTHING'S CHANGED AROUND THE OL' PARK... TRAFFIC JAMS BAD AS EVER
DON'T KNOW WHY, BUT THE RED SOX APPEAR FLAT
FENWAY PARK 1980 OPENER
PHIL PHAN
POLITICIANS OUT IN FULL FORCE AS USUAL ON OPENING DAY
EDDIE GERMANO BOSTON

PAIN IN THE NECK
I'LL TEACH YOU, YOU LI'L SQUIRT A THING OR TWO ABOUT RESPECT AND DISCIPLINE
ZIM'S WOODSHED
WAIT'LL M'LAWYER HEARS ABOUT THIS
① WHEN DON ZIMMER TOOK OVER THE RED SOX, HE WAS TO LAY THE LAW DOWN WITH HIS KIDS AND THEIR MULTI-YEAR CONTRACTS...
OW!
PING
SOX AT FENWAY TONIGHT AFTER A SAD ROAD TRIP
EDDIE GERMANO
② BUT POPEYE HAS FOUND OUT THAT IT'S A DIFFERENT BALL-GAME TODAY FROM THOSE DAYS WHEN HE CAME UP IN THE OLD DODGER ORGANIZATION

BURLY LITTLE GUY
IN THE OPINION OF MANY RED SOX BUFFS, THE ONE GUY THAT IS A MUST DAY IN AND DAY OUT IS RICK BURLESON
HOLD ON... I CAN CARRY YA!
RED SOX
JES DON'T GET HURT!
BACK IN 1978, AN INJURY TO RICK HAD AS MUCH TO DO WITH TH' RED SOX BLOWIN' TH' PENNANT AS ANYTHING
PHIL PHAN
EDDIE GERMANO
OL' PRO
BONG
RED SOX
A GREAT GUY 'ROUND TH' CLUB-HOUSE
THE RED SOX WERE KNOCKED FROM PILLAR TO POST FOR LETTING A PRO LIKE BOB WATSON GET AWAY...
...BUT ONE CAN'T FIND FAULT WITH THE WAY THAT TONY PEREZ HAS DONE THE JOB AT FIRST
EDDIE GERMANO

A (THREE) GRAND NIGHT!
FOR RED SOX FANS, IT'S BEEN A VERY BAD YEAR TO SAY THE LEAST... BUT THEY HAD SOMETHING TO CHEER FOR LAST NIGHT WHEN
YAZ!
...FINALLY GOT HIS BIG HIT, JUST WHEN IT APPEARED THE SUSPENSE WOULD GO ON FOREVER
3000 HITS
EDDIE GERMANO
DON'S FERVENT PRAYER
'N PLEASE MAKE MY PITCHERS PITCH... MY HITTERS HIT...'N HELP ME T'MAKE TH' RIGHT MOVES...OR...OR... WELL YA KNOW WHAT'LL HAPPEN T'ME!
THE WOLVES

GOOD LUCK ZIM

MISCALCULATION

1981-1985

New manager Ralph Houk brought a needed stability to the Sox in the early eighties, but the team still suffered from bad luck. The baseball strike of 1981, the ownership struggles, and (in 1983) their first losing season since 1966 plagued the Townies. Nevertheless, better pitching and some good trades set the stage for future greatness.

A FRIENDLY AND CANDID CHAT WITH RED SOX EXECUTIVE VICE-PRESIDENT EDWARD G. (BUDDY) LEROUX
WE HATED TO LOSE BURLESON, LYNN AND FISK ALL QUALITY PLAYERS, WE FEEL OUR OFFERS WERE FAIR AND SUBSTANTIAL AND COMPETITIVE IN TODAY'S MARKET
SOX
THEY LOVE ME!
OUR PITCHING COULD BE A KEY FACTOR THIS YEAR WE FEEL IT WILL BE A BETTER STAFF... THOSE WHO CAN'T CONTRIBUTE WILL BE LET GO
THE RED SOX NEED TO DRAW 2 MILLION FANS TO BE IN A SOLID POSITION FINANCIALLY... IF WE HAVE A WINNER THIS GOAL CAN BE REACHED
SUITS ME FINE
TAKE ME OUT T'TH' BALL GAME
DESPITE ADVERSE PUBLICITY OUR SURVEYS SHOW THE FANS ARE IN OUR CORNER... MAIL HAS RUN 8 OR 9 TO ONE IN OUR FAVOR... TICKET SALES ARE DOING WELL ALSO
BY 1982 WE WILL HAVE ADDED TWO THOUSAND MORE SEATS AT FENWAY, WE MAY GO TO SEVEN THOUSAND OVERALL IN NEW SEATS TO BRING THE CAPACITY OF FENWAY UP TO ABOUT 41,000
FENWAY'S LOOK WILL REMAIN THE SAME INCLUDING THE FRIENDLY GREEN MONSTER IN LEFT FIELD
EDDIE GERMANO WINTER HAVEN, FLA.

THE TWO OLDEST PLAYERS ON THE RED SOX ROSTER ARE GREY-BEARDS...

TONY PEREZ...
(39 YEARS)

and...

...YAZ...
(41 YEARS)

BETWEEN THEM THEY TOTAL...

80 YEARS!

THEY'RE ALMOST ELIGIBLE FOR SOCIAL SECURITY!

DESPITE THEIR ADVANCED YEARS FOR BASEBALL THEY ARE AMONG THE HARDEST WORKERS IN THE RED SOX CAMP

EDDIE GERMANO, WINTER HAVEN, FLA.

NEW RED SOX MANAGER RALPH HOUK HAS PITCHERS COMING OUT OF HIS EARS WITH 21 IN CAMP

AND I ONLY NEED ABOUT TEN OF 'EM

A YEAR AGO THE PITCHING BE-LONGED OUT IN THE REFUSE PILE

THE QUESTION IS HOW WELL WILL THE VETERANS BOUNCE BACK... AND CAN ANY OF THE YOUNG ARMS MAKE IT... TIME WILL TELL

EDDIE GERMANO, WINTER HAVEN, FLA.

SOMETHING'S GOTTA GIVE

YER OUT BABY!
THE GUY CAN HIT... ESPECIALLY IN CLUTCH SITUATIONS
ALL LAST WINTER THE NAME OF DWIGHT EVANS CONSTANTLY CAME UP IN TRADE TALK... THE RED SOX AS WELL AS THEIR FANS ARE SURE GLAD DEWEY IS STILL AROUND... THE GUY'S BEEN JUST SHORT OF SENSATIONAL
THERE IS NO BETTER FIELDING RIGHT FIELDER IN THE AMERICAN LEAGUE
HIS RIFLE ARM IS DEADLY AND RIGHT ON TARGET
HIS HUSTLE IS A JOY TO BEHOLD
FRANKLY I WOULDN'T TRADE HIM FOR REGGIE JACKSON!
PHIL PHAN
EDDIE GERMANO
FANS HAD A FIELD DAY GETTING AUTOGRAPHS
POW
JIM RICE HIT SHOTS OVER EVERYTHING
HANDS THAT WERE ONCE CALLOUSED ARE NOW SORE AND TENDER
TRAINER CHARLIE MOSS, BILL CAMPBELL, CARNEY LANSFORD AND STEVE CRAWFORD SPORTING BEARDS
HAYWOOD SULLIVAN, HAPPY TO BE BACK
TIME OUT FOR A BREAK OR TOTAL COLLAPSE
WHERE'S SINATRA?
IMAGINE, WILLIE NELSON AND JACKSON BROWN BLARING OUT OVER THE FENWAY SPEAKERS
THE CLUB APPEARED IN GOOD SPIRITS WITHOUT ANIMOSITY
PUFF
THE WIND SPRINTS IN 85° PLUS WEATHER IS MOST GRUELING
RALPH HOUK IS VERY PLEASED WITH THE CONDITIONING OF HIS PITCHERS
EDDIE GERMANO at FENWAY PARK

A LOT OF ATTENTION AT TOMORROWS HOME OPENER WILL BE DIRECTED AT THE FIVE FORMER ANGELS WHO HAVE FLUNG AWAY THEIR HALOS FOR THE SURROUNDINGS OF FENWAY
WE'RE HAYWOOD'S RINGERS
JOE RUDI
MARK CLEAR
FRANK TANANA
RICK MILLER
CARNEY LANSFORD
EDDIE GERMANO

WELL I'LL BE
10th PLAYER IN MAJOR LEAGUE HISTORY TO ACCUMULATE 5,000 TOTAL BASES
NO DOUBT YAZ COUL
ADD MORE RECORD
TO HIS DISTINGUIS
CAREER... BUT I ST
WOULD LIKE TO S
HIM BOW OUT A
THIS SEASON
STILL PRODUCT
RATHER THAN
ON TOO LONG
EDDIE GERMANO

1982

RALPH HOUK CLAIMS HE'S SET WITH HIS FIRST THREE STARTERS... MIKE TORREZ WHO WAS 10-3 LAST YEAR...
BOB OJEDA... 1981'S ROOKIE SENSATION WHO MANY PEOPLE CLAIM COULD WIN 20 IN 1982...
AND DENNIS ECKERSLEY WHO HAS BEEN DISAPPOINTING THE PAST TWO SEASONS
I DO IT ALL FOR YOU
FREE PASSES
YER NOT GONNA SCARE ME!
BOBBY'S BIGGEST PROBLEM WILL BE FACING THE SOPHOMORE JINX, HE'S YOUNG AND STRONG COULD BE THE ACE OF THE STAFF IN '82
THIS'S A PARTIAL LIST OF THINGS WRONG WITH ME
NOT A DURABLE KIND, THE ECK HAS HAD HIS PHYSICAL PROBLEMS, ALSO NEEDS TO GET HIS HEAD SCREWED ON STRAIGHT
IS IT YOU?
HOUK IS LOOKING FOR A FOURTH STARTER DOWN HERE RAINEY OR ONE OF THE ROOKIES COULD BE IT
EDDIE GERMANO WINTER HAVEN, FLA.

WELL I'LL BE

10th PLAYER IN MAJOR LEAGUE HISTORY TO ACCUMULATE 5,000 TOTAL BASES

NO DOUBT YAZ COULD ADD MORE RECORDS TO HIS DISTINGUISHED CAREER...BUT I STILL WOULD LIKE TO SEE HIM BOW OUT AFTER THIS SEASON WHILE STILL PRODUCTIVE... RATHER THAN HANG ON TOO LONG

EDDIE GERMANO

1982

RALPH HOUK CLAIMS HE'S SET WITH HIS FIRST THREE STARTERS... MIKE TORREZ WHO WAS 10-3 LAST YEAR...
BOB OJEDA... 1981'S ROOKIE SENSATION WHO MANY PEOPLE CLAIM COULD WIN 20 IN 1982...
AND DENNIS ECKERSLEY WHO HAS BEEN DISAPPOINTING THE PAST TWO SEASONS
I DO IT ALL FOR YOU
FREE PASSES
MIKE'S BIGGEST PROBLEM HAS BEEN HIS WILDNESS IN EARLY INNINGS, HE IMPROVED THIS FLAW LAST YEAR, SOX NEED 15 GAMES FROM HIM IN 1982
YER NOT GONNA SCARE ME!
BOBBY'S BIGGEST PROBLEM WILL BE FACING THE SOPHOMORE JINX, HE'S YOUNG AND STRONG COULD BE THE ACE OF THE STAFF IN '82
THIS'S A PARTIAL LIST OF THINGS WRONG WITH ME
NOT A DURABLE KIND, THE ECK HAS HAD HIS PHYSICAL PROBLEMS, ALSO NEEDS TO GET HIS HEAD SCREWED ON STRAIGHT
IS IT YOU?
SOX
HOUK IS LOOKING FOR A FOURTH STARTER DOWN HERE RAINEY OR ONE OF THE ROOKIES COULD BE IT
EDDIE GERMANO WINTER HAVEN, FLA.

RALPH HOUK
STARTS HIS SECOND SEASON AS RED SOX MANAGER, SO FAR HE LIKES WHAT HE SEES DOWN HERE AND IS OVERFLOWING WITH OPTIMISM
HE'S HIGH ON HIS PITCHING BOTH THE STARTERS AND BULLPEN
THINKS THAT GLENN HOFFMAN WILL FINALLY SHOW WHAT HE CAN DO AT SHORT
CONSIDERS HIS OUTFIELD ONE OF THE LEAGUE'S BEST WITH RICE BETTER THAN GIVEN CREDIT FOR
FIGURES THE INFIELD AND CATCHING ADEQUATE EVEN THOUGH STAPLETON IS LEARNING TO PLAY FIRST... I, AS YET, DON'T SHARE HOUK'S OPTIMISTIC VIEWS FOR 1982... MAYBE I'LL CHANGE MY MIND LATER AFTER MORE GRAPEFRUIT ACTION.
EDDIE GERMANO... WINTER HAVEN, FLA.

SPRING TRAINING IS MANY THINGS BESIDES JUST PLAYING BASEBALL... THERE IS ALSO THE HUMAN SIDE AS WELL...

WHERE'S TH' SUN?

THOSE WHO HAVE NO OTHER INTEREST BUT THE WEATHER

GREETING OLD FRIEND JOHNNY PESKY WHO WAS AILING AND NOW ON THE MEND

PLAYERS CARRYING THE SHOPPING AT THE WINTER HAVEN MALL

LISTENING TO RED SOX BROADCASTER KEN COLEMAN TELL HIS IRISH STORIES AT POOLSIDE

WATCHING TED WILLIAMS WATCHING WORK-OUTS

EDDIE GERMANO, WINTER HAVEN, FLA.

A YEAR AGO... DWIGHT EVANS HAD THE BEST SEASON OF HIS BIG LEAGUE CAREER
THE SHOTS I'VE SEEN HIM HIT SO FAR DOWN HERE WOULD INDICATE HE'S OUT TO DUPLICATE LAST YEAR'S STATS
MAKES US PAUNCHY GUYS GREEN WITH ENVY!
DEWEY IS POSITIVELY IN THE BEST SHAPE OF HIS CAREER
EDDIE GERMANO, WINTER HAVEN, FLA.
HOPING TO BE THE SECOND BIRD TO FLY OVER THE HUB'S SPORTS SKY-LINE IS MARK FIDRYCH
NO MATTER WHERE HE GOES DOWN HERE HE IS THE CENTER OF ATTENTION
HE'S 27 NOW WITH A KID'S ENTHUSIASM... EVEN ENJOYS DOING WIND-SPRINTS
I'LL PITCH BATTIN' PRACTISE
EASY... EASY!
UNDER THE WATCHFUL EYE OF PITCHING COACH LEE STANGE MARK IS THROWING EASY
WE ARE PLEASED WITH HIS PROGRESS BUT HE HASN'T OPENED UP YET AND WILL NOT DO SO UNTIL WE'RE SURE, EVEN IF IT TAKES ALL YEAR
ARTHUR PAPPAS, TEAM DR.
GOT A STANDING 'O' JUST WALKING ACROSS THE FIELD IN LAKELAND
EDDIE GERMANO, WINTER HAVEN, FLA.

CARNEY LANSFORD WAS THE LAST RED SOX PLAYER TO WIN THE A.L. BATTING TITLE WITH A .336... BUT THE WAY
WADE BOGGS
IS KNOCKING PITCHERS AROUND...HE COULD VERY WELL BE THE NEXT
MAYBE RALPH HOUK SHOULD PUT THE ENTIRE BALL CLUB ON A CHICKEN DIET!
PHIL PHAN
I RATE AN ASSIST TOO!
EDDIE GERMANO
HAYWOOD SULLIVAN
YAWKEY WAY
HOUK PEACHES 9 FOR A $1.00
25¢
YAZ PLUMS $1.00 lb
EVANS ZUCCHINI 50¢
RICE PATTIES
LANSFORD LEMONS
ECK 75¢ CUCUMBERS
RED SOX SPECIALS
EDDIE GERMANO

1983

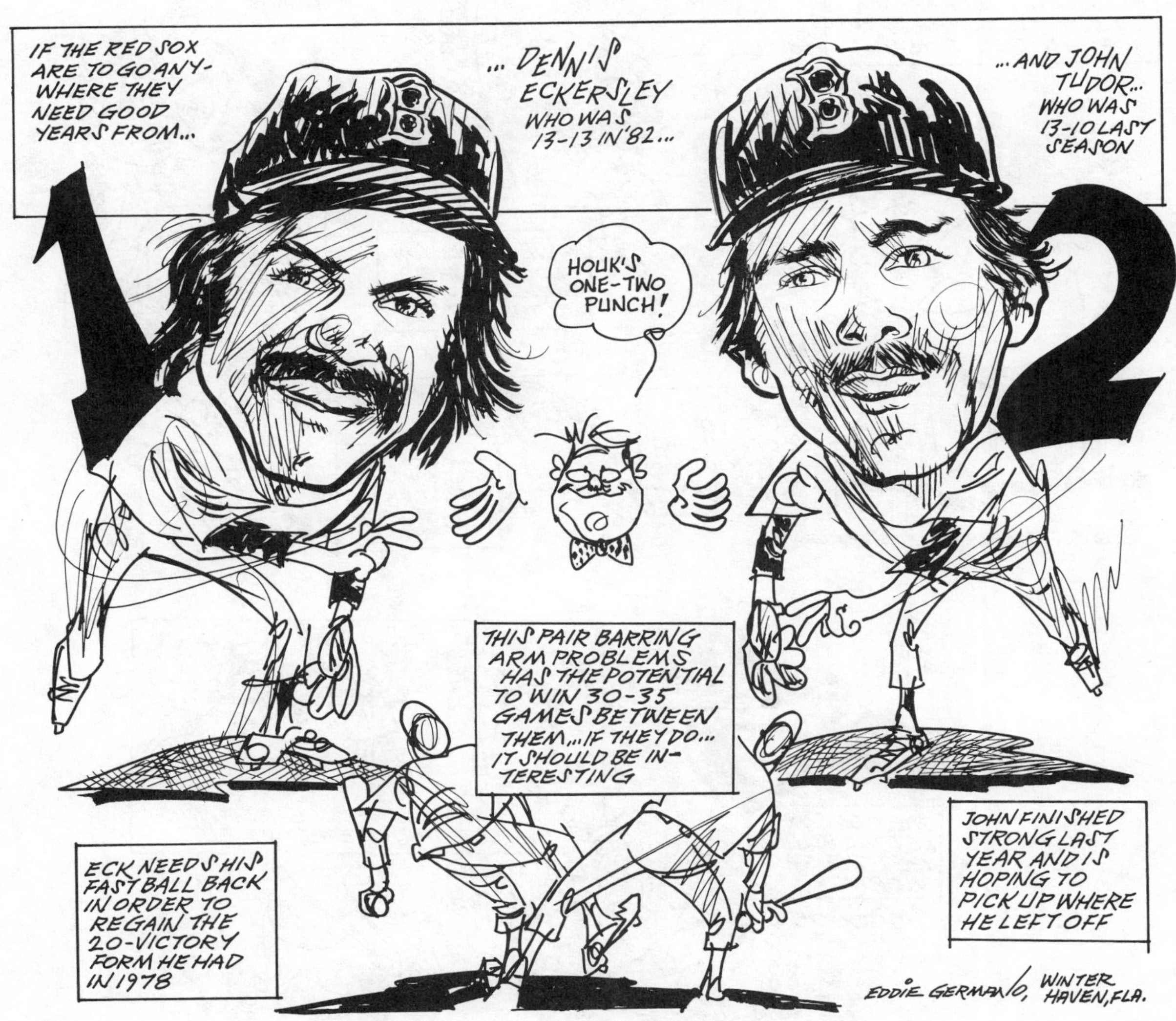

IF THE RED SOX ARE TO GO ANYWHERE THEY NEED GOOD YEARS FROM...
...DENNIS ECKERSLEY WHO WAS 13-13 IN '82...
...AND JOHN TUDOR... WHO WAS 13-10 LAST SEASON
1
2
HOUK'S ONE-TWO PUNCH!
THIS PAIR BARRING ARM PROBLEMS HAS THE POTENTIAL TO WIN 30-35 GAMES BETWEEN THEM,...IF THEY DO... IT SHOULD BE INTERESTING
ECK NEEDS HIS FASTBALL BACK IN ORDER TO REGAIN THE 20-VICTORY FORM HE HAD IN 1978
JOHN FINISHED STRONG LAST YEAR AND IS HOPING TO PICK UP WHERE HE LEFT OFF
EDDIE GERMANO, WINTER HAVEN, FLA.

THE RED SOX OPENED THEIR SEASON YESTERDAY ON A SOUR NOTE LOSING TO THE TORONTO BLUE JAYS 7-1
IT'S YUMMY !
GIVE A CHEER
POW
BURP !
RED SOX
DAVE STAPLETON CLOCKED THE LONE SOX RUN IN THE NETS
TWICE THE SOX HAD BASES LOADED... BUT COULDN'T GET THE KEY HIT
THE JAYS FEASTED ON THE OFFERINGS OF... DENNIS ECKERSLEY
HOMERS BY UPSHAW AND MULLINIKS DID THE ECK IN
RED SOX BATS WERE MADE OF PUTTY
EDDIE GERMANO at FENWAY PARK
GLUB GLUB
HOLD IT!
BOTH BENCHES CLEARED WHEN RICE THREATENED STIEB
THE RED SOX LET THE BLUE JAYS GET THE EARLY WORM
FENWAY'S NEW LIGHT TOWERS ADDED BRIGHT-NESS TO A DULL DAY
YAZ GOT A BIG HAND AS EXPECTED WHEN HE CAME TO THE PLATE
BRUCE HURST AND JOHN HENRY JOHNSON TURNED IN GOOD RELIEF WORK

PEOPLE TALK ABOUT THE HITTING POTENTIAL OF THE RED SOX...NO ARGUMENT THERE...
RIGHT...
LEFT
THE PITCHING IS A BIG QUESTION, MADE WEAKER BY WHAT I THINK WILL BE A POOR INFIELD...
EDDIE GERMANO
BOGGS IS STILL LEARNING TO PLAY 3RD
HOFFMAN AT SHORT, COMING OFF KNEE SURGERY
RED SOX INFIELD
IF THE INFIELD LOOKS LIKE SWISS CHEESE YOU CAN SEE WHY AND A GOOD DEFENSE IS A MUST IN ORDER TO WIN
REMY'S GIMPY LEGS
STAPLETON'S VERSATILE BUT STILL NOT A NATURAL AT 1ST
I'LL HAVE SOME WITH CRACKERS 'N A GLASS OF ROSE'
PHIL PHAN

SOMETHING TO SEE...
BRUCE HURST...
THE STYLISH RED SOX LEFTY HAS LOOKED SUPERB IN HIS INITIAL STARTS AND LOOKS LIKE A POTENTIAL 20-GAME WINNER BARRING INJURIES...
...HE'S HAD ENEMY HITTERS TALKING TO THEM-SELVES
WE'RE ON AN UPBEAT!
RED SOX PITCHING
... BRUCE IS GIVING THE CLUB'S PITCHING STAFF A TREMENDOUS LIFT AND HE MAY VERY WELL BE THE BEST LEFT-HANDER THE RED SOX HAVE HAD SINCE THE DAYS OF MEL PARNELL
EDDIE GERMANO
THE ONE THING THAT BODES WELL FOR NEXT YEAR IS THE YOUNG PITCHING STAFF THE RED SOX HAVE GOING...
LULLABY 'N GOOD NIGHT...
YOU'VE BEEN PITCHIN' ALL RIGHT...
JUST REMEMBER, T'THROW STRIKES...
'CAUSE THAT'S WHAT HOUK LIKES...
...AND NOT TOO MUCH CREDIT CAN BE GIVEN TO PITCHING COACH LEE STANGE WHO HAS NURSED THE YOUNG ARMS TO PERFECTION
EDDIE GERMANO

A PROFILE
RALPH HOUK TOOK OVER FROM DON ZIMMER IN 1980, IT WAS CONSIDERED A GOOD MOVE AT THAT TIME...
NOW WITH THE CLUB FLOUNDERING I BELIEVE A CHANGE IS IN ORDER STARTING WITH THE MANAGER..
NOW, DON'T SAY ANYTHING NEGATIVE ABOUT TH' MAJOR!
HOUK HAS HAD A PHENOMENAL PRESS CORP RAPPORT WITH LITTLE OR NO CRITICISM EVEN WHEN IT'S DESERVED...
BEFORE ANOTHER SEASON ROLLS AROUND, I'D LIKE TO SEE A NEW MANAGER AND THE TRADING OF ONE OF THE OUTFIELDERS IN A PACKAGE FOR SOME SPEED TO GO WITH THAT YOUNG PITCHING-
EDDIE GERMANO

WISHING WELL
I WISH I COULD GET OUT OF THIS MESS
RED SOX
A.L. EAST
EDDIE GERMANO
THANKS FOR THE MEMORIES YAZ
8
WHERE DID TH' TIME GO?
PHIL PHAN
EDDIE GERMANO

1984

THE ETERNAL OPTIMIST
"I LOOK FOR ECKERSLEY AND CLEAR TO MAKE FINE COMEBACKS"
"RICE, ARMAS AND EVANS... IS THERE A BETTER OUT-FIELD?"
"ALL WE NEED IS A FEW BREAKS AND STAY AWAY FROM INJURIES"
"OUR INFIELD IS BETTER, OUR BENCH IS MUCH STRONGER, OUR CATCHING WILL BE OK"
"MIKE EASLER IS GOING TO BE A BIG PLUS"
GOOD OL' RALPH HOUK, HE SURE CAN BUILD UP YER HOPES, EVEN THOUGH WE KNOW DIFFERENT
PHIL PHAN
RALPH HOUK... IF THE PENNANT RACE WAS TO BE DECIDED ON OPTIMISM... HIS RED SOX SHOULD WIN THE FLAG BY 20 GAMES
EDDIE GERMANO

ON THEIR MERRY WAY
NOW DON'T GO TOO FAST...I DON'T WANT TH' WIND TO MESS UP MY HAIR
RED SOX SLOW '84 START
YOU DON'T HAVE T'WORRY 'BOUT IT!
EDDIE GERMANO

BOSTON RED SOX
1967
AMERICAN LEAGUE
CHAMPIONS

67

PHIL PHAN

LAST NIGHT'S TRIBUTE TO TONY C., AND THE INTRODUCTION OF PLAYERS FROM THE 1967 MIRACLE RED SOX CAUSED MANY A NOSTALGIC TEAR TO BE SHED BY BOSTON FANDOM AT FRIENDLY FENWAY

EDDIE GERMANO

ME AND MY SHADOW
INJURY JINX
RED SOX
WESTERN BADLANDS
EDDIE GERMANO

ONE THAT GOT AWAY
RED SOX
JOHN TUDOR
EDDIE GERMANO

YEA RED SOX... ...WITH ALL THOSE YOUNG ARMS... WE'RE GONNA BE ROLLIN'...
WHO CARES WHO OWNS TH' TEAM...LET THEM SETTLE THAT IN COURT...
...I'M JUST GONNA GO OUT THERE EVERY DAY 'N DO TH' JOB OF WINNING BALL GAMES...
OOPS!
LUCKY F'ME YOU'RE HERE!
UGH!
CLEVELAND
A.L. EAST CELLAR
EDDIE GERMANO
NIGHTMARES
THE CHAMPION DETROIT TIGERS PROVED THEY'RE THE BEST AND ALREADY THE RED SOX ARE HAVING SLEEPLESS NIGHTS WORRYING ABOUT HOW TO BEAT THEM OUT NEXT YEAR
RED SOX
EDDIE GERMANO

TIME TO GET OFF THE DUFF
THEY SAY MOVES AND TRADES DEVELOP AT WORLD SERIES TIME... AND WORLD SERIES TIME IS ALMOST HERE, KIDDIES
WHO ME?
RED SOX
RUMORS AND CONJECTURE
EDDIE GERMANO

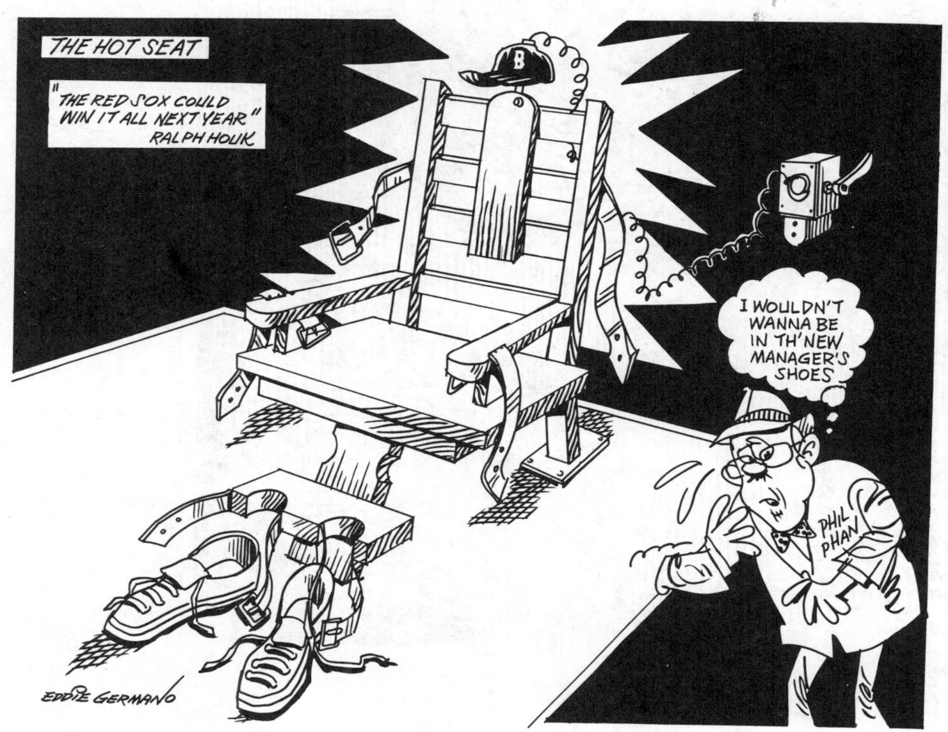
THE HOT SEAT
"THE RED SOX COULD WIN IT ALL NEXT YEAR." RALPH HOUK
I WOULDN'T WANNA BE IN TH' NEW MANAGER'S SHOES
PHIL PHAN
EDDIE GERMANO

1985

JOHN McNAMARA RUMORED TO BE NEW RED SOX MANAGER — NEWS
OH ME NAME IS McNAMARA I'M THE LEADER OF THE BAND...
... AND IF YOU DON'T WIN THE PENNANT YOUR HEAD WILL BE IN DEMAND
THE FANS
THIS IS THE YEAR!
THE FUTURE IS NOW
RED SOX IN 1985
RED SOX
EDDIE GERMANO

WINTER HAVEN SKETCH-BOOK
NEW PITCHING COACH BILL FISCHER LIKES CONTROL ON THE PART OF THE STAFF AND IS WORKING HARD TO IMPROVE THE BASES ON BALLS DEPT.
BOYS'LL BE BOYS!
LAND SAKES... WHAT ARE YOU WHIPPER SNAPPERS UP TO?
AMERICAN LEAGUE
BRUCE HURST
ROGER CLEMENS
BOBBY OJEDA
OIL CAN BOYD
AL NIPPER WHEN HE RECOVERS
MA McNAMARA HAS A POTENTIAL STARTING FIVE THAT AVERAGES ABOUT 25 YEARS UNLESS IT'S DECIDED TO MAKE ONE A RELIEVER
THESE YOUNG GUYS COULD BE A FEISTY AND PESTY BUNCH AROUND THE A.L. THIS SEASON WITH THE POTENTIAL TO WIN BIG
EDDIE GERMANO, W-H FLORIDA

A REMINDER
I'M AN ALL-STAR! I'M AN ALL-STAR! I'M AN...
OIL CAN
THUMP
THUMP
*THUMP
WHAT'S GOIN' ON UP THERE? HOW'S A GUY GONNA GET ANY SLEEP?
SPARKY ANDERSON
EDDIE GERMANO

REST YE MERRY GENTLEMEN
NO. 1 STAR
BUDDY
SULLY
RED SOX
WISH YOU GUYS WOULD GET THINGS RESOLVED SOON BEFORE EVERY-THING TOPPLES DOWN
PHIL PHAN
EDDIE GERMANO

HARD TIME HOLDING RUNNERS ON BASE
HIGH EARNED-RUN AVERAGE
CONTROL
THE LONG BALL
INABILITY TO HOLD LEADS
THE DAYS HAVEN'T BEEN SO CLEAR FOR MARK CLEAR AND HE IS ONE OF THE REASONS WHY THE RED SOX HAVE ENCOUNTERED SO MUCH STORMY WEATHER THIS SEASON
B
SOX
RAIN DROPS FALLIN' ON M'HEAD... EVEN WITH TH' DROUGHT
PHIL PHAN
EDDIE GERMANO
RAMPAGING IN REVERSE
RED SOX BULLPEN CREW
YOU'RE SUPPOSED TO GO AFTER ENEMY HITTERS... NOT ME !
McNAMARA
EDDIE GERMANO

WINTER HAVEN SKETCHBOOK
TONY ARMAS
HE BOUNCED BACK FROM A DISMAL .218 BA IN 1983 TO .268 AND HOPES TO IMPROVE ON THAT MARK IN 1985
THE RED SOX BRASS THINK OF TONY AS A COMPLETE PRO WHO SETS HIS OWN PACE DOWN HERE
LED THE MAJORS WITH 43 HOMERS LAST YEAR... FLORIDA IS ROUTINE FOR TONY SINCE HAILING FROM VENEZUELA ITS BASEBALL ALL YEAR LONG
THE RED SOX HAVE HAD SOME GREAT CENTER FIELDERS AND I DON'T CONSIDER TONY ONE OF THE BETTER ONES BUT HE'S ADEQUATE
ARMAS, RICE, EVANS & EASLER PROVIDE SOME SOLID OFFENSE... BUT I'D LIKE TO SEE HIM CUT DOWN MORE ON HIS K'S... TONY WOULD TOO
EDDIE GERMANO
W-H, FLORIDA
INTO THE SUNSET
1985 RED SOX
AND WHEN YA COME BACK NEXT YEAR... BRING ALONG SOME NEW FACES... ESPECIALLY RELIEF PITCHERS!
PHIL PHAN
EDDIE GERMANO
THE ENTERPRISE

1986

1986 was a year of superlatives for the Red Sox. Early in the season the dazzling Roger Clemens set a new strikeout record (20). He also won his first fourteen games, finished the season 24-4, and won both the MVP and Cy Young awards. The efforts of Clemens and others brought the Sox once again to the World Series, this time against the Mets. Alas, history repeated itself.

ARBITRARILY SPEAKING
RED SOX GM LOU GORMAN SAYS HE ISN'T CONCERNED ABOUT THE LIST OF SOX PLAYERS WHO HAVE FILED FOR ARBITRATION
THINK I'LL GIVE LOU ANOTHER HOT FOOT FROM TH' HOT CORNER
WADE BOGGS
BUT THE GUY HEADING THAT LIST WON A COOL MILLION LAST YEAR AND IS LOOKING FOR DOUBLE THAT NOW
EDDIE GERMANO

WINTER HAVEN SKETCHBOOK
JINX
I'M KEEPIN' MY SCALPEL WITH THE REST OF MY BASEBALL MEMORABILIA
THE INJURY JINX HAS HAMPERED ROGER SINCE COMING INTO THE MAJOR LEAGUES
the DOCS
ROGER CLEMENS
ATTEMPTING TO COME BACK FROM SURGERY
BOTH PITCHERS CAN BE MIGHTY IMPORTANT TO THE RED SOX IF THEY ARE SOUND PHYSICALLY
WHERE IS IT?
ZOOM
THE BIG "IF" IF THESE TWO ARE BACK TO FORM THERE WILL BE SOME FUN THIS YEAR
ROGER CAN THROW HARD WITH THE BEST WHEN HE IS PAIN FREE AND HE SAYS HE IS
BOB STANLEY
HE OWNS THE CLUB RECORD FOR SAVES WITH 107 AND HOPES TO ADD MANY MORE
GLUB GLUB
OPPOSITION
the STANLEY SINKER
EDDIE GERMANO WINTER HAVEN FLA.

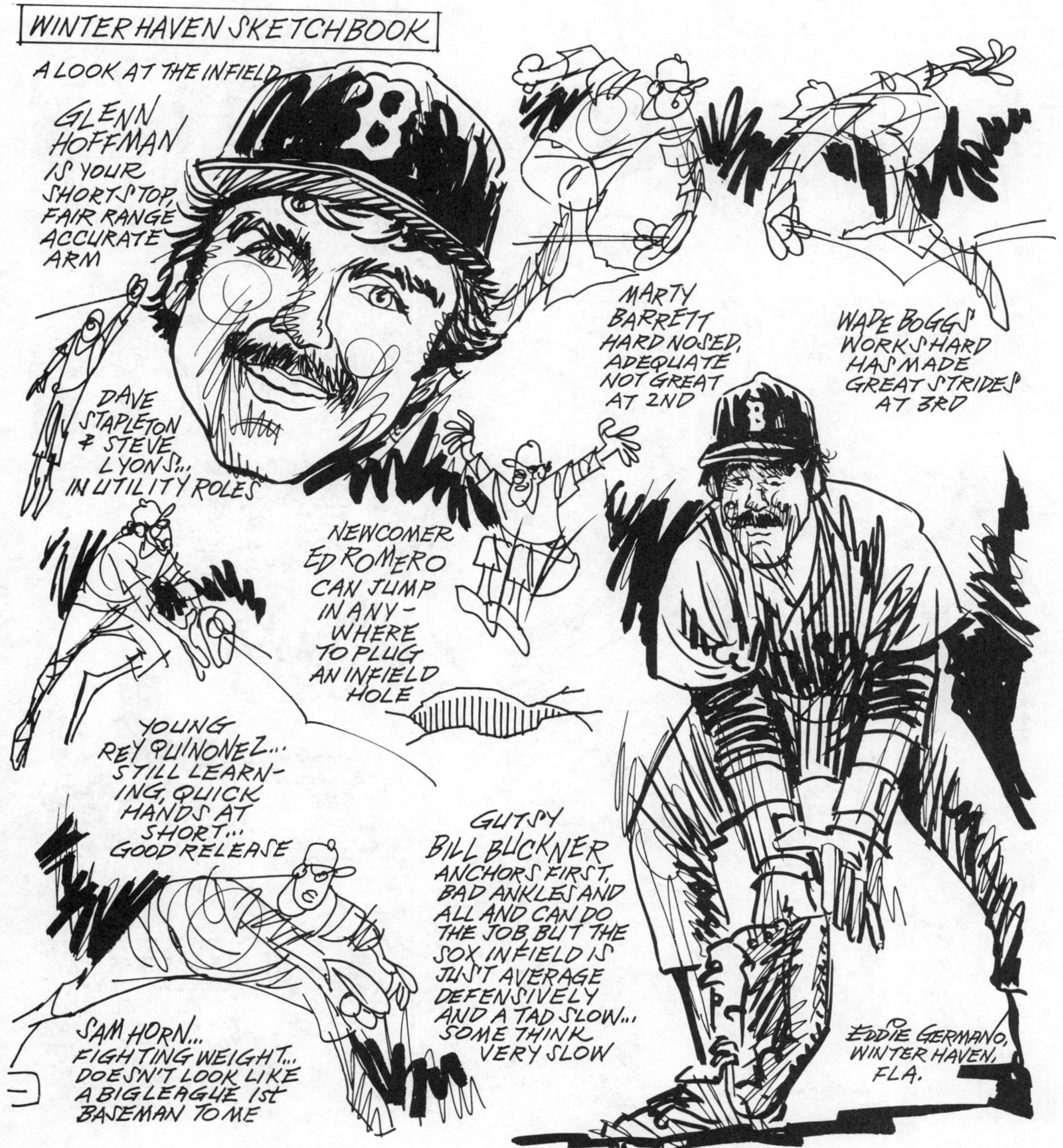
WINTER HAVEN SKETCHBOOK
A LOOK AT THE INFIELD
GLENN HOFFMAN IS YOUR SHORTSTOP, FAIR RANGE ACCURATE ARM
MARTY BARRETT HARD NOSED, ADEQUATE NOT GREAT AT 2ND
WADE BOGGS WORKS HARD HAS MADE GREAT STRIDES AT 3RD
DAVE STAPLETON & STEVE LYONS... IN UTILITY ROLES
NEWCOMER ED ROMERO CAN JUMP IN ANY-WHERE TO PLUG AN INFIELD HOLE
YOUNG REY QUINONEZ... STILL LEARN-ING, QUICK HANDS AT SHORT... GOOD RELEASE
GUTSY BILL BUCKNER ANCHORS FIRST, BAD ANKLES AND ALL AND CAN DO THE JOB BUT THE SOX INFIELD IS JUST AVERAGE DEFENSIVELY AND A TAD SLOW... SOME THINK VERY SLOW
SAM HORN... FIGHTING WEIGHT... DOESN'T LOOK LIKE A BIG LEAGUE 1st BASEMAN TO ME
EDDIE GERMANO, WINTER HAVEN, FLA.

WINTER HAVEN SKETCHBOOK
MANAGER JOHN McNAMARA TALKS ABOUT HIS BALL CLUB...
"I'VE HAD SEVERAL TEAM MEETINGS AND THE PLAYERS HAVE BEEN TOLD WHAT I EXPECT OF THEM SUCH AS LEAVING YOUR PROBLEMS AT HOME AND BE READY TO PLAY BALL"
"I'VE KNOWN ABOUT THE COUNTRY CLUB IMAGE ON THIS CLUB... IT'S GONNA CHANGE... BELIEVE ME"
"I WAS RAISED A POOR IRISH KID OUT OF SACRAMENTO, CAL., AND HAD TO PROVE MYSELF EVERY DAY"
JOHN McNAMARA
"WE DON'T HAVE GREAT SPEED BUT WE'LL BE MORE AGRESSIVE ON THE BASES"
KNOCK
KNOCK
"I WAS EXTREMELY DISAPPOINTED IN THE 1985 SEASON, WE SHOULD HAVE DONE BETTER"
"MY DOOR IS OPEN TO ANYONE WHO'S GOT A BEEF... WE WANT THINGS OUT IN THE OPEN"
"I'M GIVING OUR KIDS A FAIR CHANCE DOWN HERE"
"I HONESTLY BELIEVE WE ARE IMPROVED OVER LAST YEAR... THE PLAYERS HAVE TO REALIZE YOU JUST CAN'T THROW YOUR GLOVE ON THE FIELD YOU HAVE TO WORK AT IT"
EDDIE GERMANO, WINTER HAVEN, FLA.

SPRING TRAINING SKETCHBOOK
THE RED SOX CAN BOAST OF HAVING TWO OF THE BEST PITCHERS IN BASEBALL
RED SOX
BRUCE HURST... AND...
...OIL CAN BOYD
30-40
IF BOTH CAN STAY HEALTHY AND IF THE CAN WILL ATTEND TO BUSINESS... THERE IS THE POTENTIAL OF 30-40 WINS BETWEEN THEM
TH' CAN, CAN AND WILL!
WHEN THE CAN'S IN A TALKING MOOD HE CAN BE REGALING
EDDIE GERMANO WINTER HAVEN, FLA.
WORK OF ART
TOM SEAVER
RED SOX G.M. LOU GORMAN
EDDIE GERMANO

FRONT OFFICE SQUABBLE
RED SOX
EDDIE GERMANO

RED SOX
THE SUMMER DOG DAYS
PENNANT TRAIL
GRRRRR
EDDIE GERMANO

HUMPTY DUMPTY?
B
RED SOX
FIRST PLACE
NOW, YOU BE CAREFUL UP THERE... REMEMBER 1978!
PHIL PHAN
EDDIE GERMANO

GO FOR IT!
RED SOX
AMERICAN LEAGUE PENNANT
ANGELS
PHIL PHAN
EDDIE GERMANO

TODAY'S ANOTHER DAY
I'M REALLY NO ANGEL!
MIKE WITT STOOD THE SOX ON THEIR HEADS
MARVIN MARVIN MARVIN
CHAMP MARVIN HAGLER WAS ON HAND
MARTY BARRETT HAD TWO BINGLES
ROGER CLEMENS JUST DIDN'T HAVE IT LAST NIGHT
BLANKETS WERE IN ORDER
OL' PAL RICK BURLESON PINCHED HIT
BOO
BOO
BOO
BOO
BOB STANLEY GOT HIS USUAL GREETING
RUNS
DOUG DECINCES SPARKLED AT 3RD
THE ANGELS' BIG 2ND INNING DID IT
EDDIE GERMANO at FENWAY

BACK ON THE WINNING TRACK
WHAT IF WE LOSE AGAIN?
OH MY!
THE FANS WERE FEARING THE WORST... NOT TO WORRY
EVANS SPARKLED ON JOYNER
OOPS
BOTH CLUBS PLAYED LIKE LI'L LEAGUERS...
SOX HAD McCASKILL ON THE ROPES EARLY
IN THE 4TH THE ANGELS' DEFENSE SPRUNG LEAKS
I CAN'T STAND BEACHBALLS AND KNUCKLE-HEAD FANS
BRUCE HURST PITCHED WELL ENOUGH TO WIN
9-2
VICTORY
WALLY JOYNER PARKED ONE...
...JIM RICE DID THE SAME TOO
CALIFORNIA HERE I COME
RED SOX
THE SOX ARE NOW OFF TO THE WEST COAST
EDDIE GERMANO at FENWAY

SOUND ADVICE
GO WEST YOUNG MAN!
THE RED SOX TOOK HORACE GREELEY'S ADVICE AND HEADED WEST...TWO OUT OF THREE FROM THE ANGELS WOULD BE JUST FINE GUYS
EDDIE GERMANO

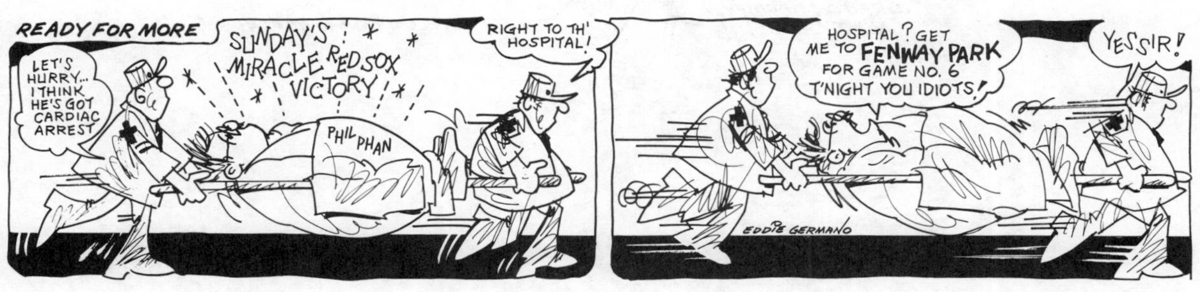
READY FOR MORE
LET'S HURRY... I THINK HE'S GOT CARDIAC ARREST
SUNDAY'S MIRACLE RED SOX VICTORY
RIGHT TO TH' HOSPITAL!
PHIL PHAN
HOSPITAL? GET ME TO FENWAY PARK FOR GAME NO. 6 T'NIGHT YOU IDIOTS!
YESSIR!
EDDIE GERMANO

ONE MORE TO GO
BUCKNER HIT A 400 ft SINGLE
I WON'T BE DENIED!
THE HOSE EXPLODED FOR FIVE RUNS IN THE THIRD AND WERE ON THEIR WAY
BANG BOOM
POW
5
THE ANGELS GOT OFF TO A FLYING START WITH TWO RUNS...
PURTY
BUT THE SOX CAME RIGHT BACK TO TIE IT
OIL CAN SETTLED DOWN AND PITCHED STEADY BALL
ANGEL PITCHING IS FAR FROM HEAVENLY
44
REGGIE IS ELECTRIFYING EVEN WHEN HE K'S
MARTY BARRETT CONTINUES WITH A HOT BAT
DOUG FLUTIE GOT LOTSA PRE-GAME MEDIA PLAY
BOSTON RED SOX 1986 A L CHAMPIONS
SPIKE OWEN'S GRAB ON DOWNEY... NIFTY
THE CAN CAUGHT GRICH'S POPUP HIMSELF
TONIGHT'S THE NIGHT!
EDDIE GERMANO at FENWAY

THE POSSIBLE DREAM COME TRUE!
BOGGS' TWO-RUN SINGLE GAVE CLEMENS A CUSHION...
...WHILE ROGER MOWED 'EM DOWN
POW!
JIM RICE'S SHOT FROSTED THE PENNANT CAKE
THE PRU GOT INTO THE SPIRIT OF THINGS
BRING ON TH' METS
8-1 VICTORY
THE NIGHT BELONGED TO ROGER CLEMENS... HE WAS SUPERB!
PENNANT
WE'RE NO.1
EVANS SCREENED ONE
BOGGS SHOWED HE CAN FIELD TOO
SCHIRALDI RELIEVED IN THE 8th...
AND THREW BULLETS AT THE FALLEN ANGELS
EDDIE GERMANO at FENWAY

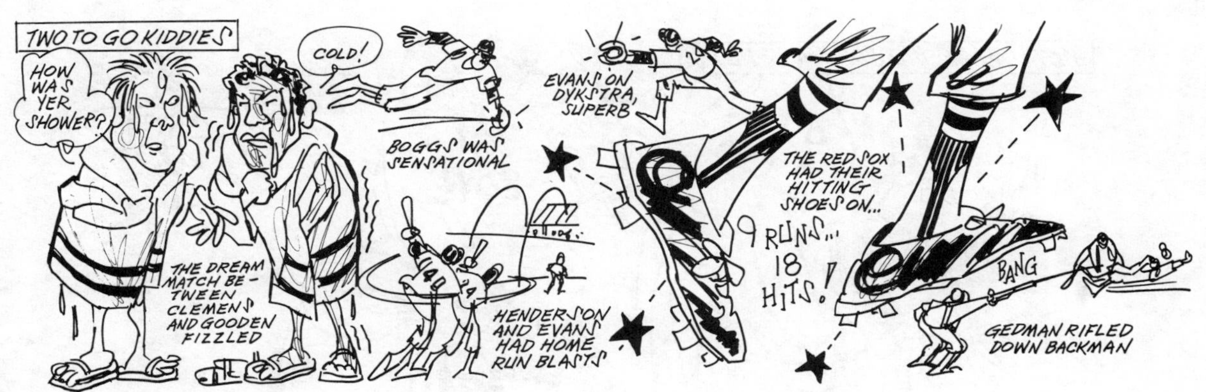
TWO TO GO KIDDIES
HOW WAS YER SHOWER?
COLD!
THE DREAM MATCH BETWEEN CLEMENS AND GOODEN FIZZLED
BOGGS WAS SENSATIONAL
EVANS ON DYKSTRA, SUPERB
HENDERSON AND EVANS HAD HOME RUN BLASTS
THE RED SOX HAD THEIR HITTING SHOES ON...
9 RUNS... 18 HITS!
BANG
GEDMAN RIFLED DOWN BACKMAN

THEY'D BE BOOIN' AT FENWAY
McNAMARA'S MOVE TO RELIEVE CRAWFORD WITH STANLEY PAID OFF
BUCKNER'S ALL SET FOR WINTER WITH HIS GALOSHES
PHIL PHAN
STILL EARLY FOR CHAMPAGNE... BUT HAVE IT READY
EDDIE GERMANO

WORLD SERIES GRAFFITI
I HATE NEW YORK
RED SOX
EDDIE GERMANO

METS MAKE THE SOX THEIR PETS

TAKE THAT 'N THAT 'N THAT!

4

POW

DYKSTRA PARKED ONE IN A HURRY

THE METS KICKED THE CAN AROUND FOR FOUR IN THE FIRST... ENOUGH TO WIN IT

RETIRING TIP O'NEILL THREW OUT THE FIRST BALL

THE SOX OFFENSE WAS LIKE BOSTON CREAM PIE

I'LL TAKE THAT!

BOB OJEDA SHOWED NO MERCY TO HIS EX TEAMMATES

7-1

WITH HERNANDEZ AND CARTER RUNNING THE SOX MESSED IT UP IN THE 1st

RED SOX

GEE

A DISAPPOINTED FENWAY CROWD FILED OUT EARLY

BACKMAN ON OWEN... STARRY

OUR GUYS PUSHED THEIR ONLY RUN ACROSS IN THE 3RD

AL NIPPER... WILL TRY TO GET THE SOX ON THE RIGHT TRACK TONIGHT

EDDIE GERMANO at FENWAY

ONE MORE TO GO!

TED WILLIAMS' THREW OUT TH' FIRST BALL

HENDERSON TRIPLED AND SCORED THE 1st RUN

IT'S MIDNIGHT... ...DO YOU KNOW WHERE YOUR PLAYERS ARE?

THESE LATE-STARTING NIGHT GAMES ARE A PAIN

HIC

AGAIN... THE SOX LEFT THE BASES LOADED IN THE 1st

STRAWBERRY IS A MELTDOWN VICTIM IN THIS SERIES

IT HURTS TO SEE BUCKNER TRY TO RUN

RED SOX

THE SOX LEFT A MESS STRANDED

FOR POST SEASON PLAY

BULLDOG BARRETT SET A NEW HIT RECORD

RICE'S TRIPLE DENTED THE BULLPEN WALL

TASTES LOUSY!

LESS FILLING!

4-2 WIN

BRUCE HURST! HAD THE METS EATING OUT OF HIS HAND

WORLD SERIES TITLE

SOX

THE RED SOX NEED ONE MORE BITE OUT OF THE BIG APPLE TO WIN IT

EDDIE GERMANO at FENWAY

WE'RE ALL EVEN

THE RED SOX LEFT THE BASES LOADED IN THE FIRST...
SITTIN' PRETTY!
AL NIPPER GAVE IT A GOOD TRY
TWO FOR TH' MONEY!
GARY CARTER HAD HIS HR SWING GOING
...AND LET RON DARLING OFF THE HOOK
SEE YA!
HOW'S YA GOLF?
GEDMAN AND NIPPER HAD MORE TALKS THAN THE U.N.
A ROCK

GO SOX
EVEN BALLOONS FROM HEAVEN DIDN'T HELP
THE HOSE APPEAR TO BE FLAT IN LOSING IT 6-2
GRR!
MARTY 'BULLDOG' BARRETT'S SWINGING A HOT BAT!
METS
RED SOX
SOX AND METS ARE NOW ALL TIED UP GOING INTO TONIGHT'S BIG ONE
EDDIE GERMANO at FENWAY
DYKSTRA'S HR WENT OFF DEWEY'S GLOVE
GEDMAN TRYING FOR A 2B IN THE 6th WAS DUMB... KILLING A RALLY
THE METS HAVE SOMETHING THE SOX DON'T HAVE... SPEED!

1987-1988

The awful finale to the 1986 World Series haunted the Sox in 1987—their record was dismal. At first, 1988 looked no better, but things changed when Manager John McNamara was replaced by longtime coach Joe Morgan. The ''Morgan Miracle'' lifted the Sox to first place in the AL East. A tough Oakland team ended their Series dreams, but all in all, it was a year to remember.

STILL ON THE TABLE

RED SOX OFFER

LOOKS MORE AND MORE TEMPTING... MAYBE I SHOULD GO FOR IT...

RICH GEDMAN

HOUSTON

OAKLAND

EDDIE GERMANO

SPRING TRAINING SKETCHBOOK
DWIGHT EVANS
THE RED SOX VETERAN FIRST PUT ON A RED SOX UNIFORM IN 1972...
1-2
1-2
A PHYSICAL FITNESS BUFF WHO WORKS HARD TO KEEP IN SHAPE
DESPITE THE YEARS... HIS ARM IS STILL TO BE FEARED
IS LOOKING FORWARD TO 1987 WITH THE ENTHUSIASM OF A ROOKIE
MANY OF THE TEENS WHO HOUND HIM FOR AUTOGRAPHS WEREN'T EVEN BORN WHEN DEWEY BROKE IN THE MAJORS
EDDIE GERMANO - WINTER HAVEN, FLA.
SPRING TRAINING SKETCHBOOK
BOB STANLEY
BOTH PITCHERS ARE WORKING HARD AND TRYING TO FORGET THE 1986 WORLD SERIES NIGHTMARE... THEY RATE HIGH IN McNAMARA'S PITCHING PLANS FOR 1987
CALVIN SCHIRALDI
EDDIE GERMANO
WINTER HAVEN, FLA.

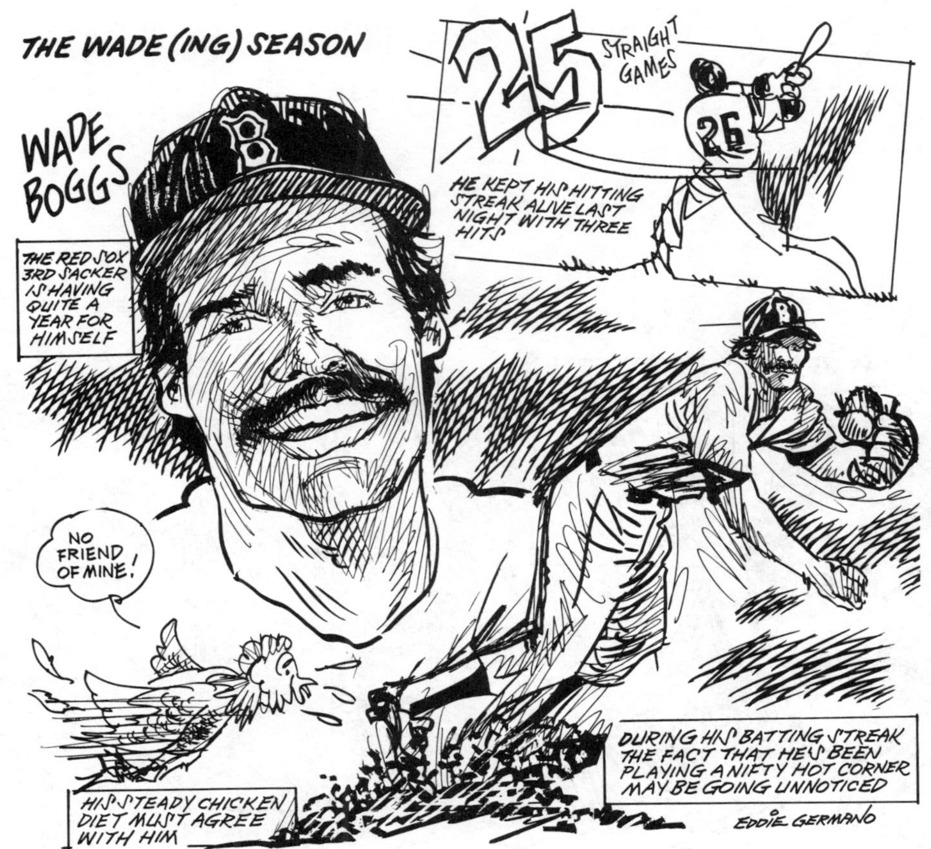
THE WADE (ING) SEASON
25 STRAIGHT GAMES
26
WADE BOGGS
HE KEPT HIS HITTING STREAK ALIVE LAST NIGHT WITH THREE HITS
THE RED SOX 3RD SACKER IS HAVING QUITE A YEAR FOR HIMSELF
NO FRIEND OF MINE!
DURING HIS BATTING STREAK THE FACT THAT HE'S BEEN PLAYING A NIFTY HOT CORNER MAY BE GOING UNNOTICED
HIS STEADY CHICKEN DIET MUST AGREE WITH HIM
EDDIE GERMANO

WHAT A DIFFERENCE A YEAR MAKES...
21
GIANTS
CARDS
TIGERS
TWINS
THE RED SOX SLOWLY WALK OUT OF THE 1987 BASEBALL PICTURE AFTER A DISMAL SEASON...
EDDIE GERMANO
... ONE OF THE CLUB'S BRIGHT LIGHTS IS OF COURSE ROGER CLEMENS... A CY YOUNG CANDIDATE...
... WE CAN NOW FOCUS OUR ATTENTION TO THE PLAY-OFFS... WITHOUT THE 1986 A.L. CHAMPION RED SOX... WHAT A DIFFERENCE A YEAR MAKES!

HE CAN BITE
HIS FIELDING HAS BEEN SOLID...
THOUGH NOT A POWER HITTER... HE DOES MAKE FINE CONTACT...
GRR
GRR
GRR
MARTY BARRETT
THE LITTLE RED SOX' 2ND SACKER IS THE HARD-NOSED TYPE WITH A LOT OF THE OLD BULLDOG IN HIM
EDDIE GERMANO

NO TIME TO LOSE

1st PLACE
HIGHWAY
A.L. N.L.

WELL, IF WE'RE GONNA MEET AGAIN IN TH' WORLD SERIES, WE'D BETTER GET MOVIN'!

mets

RED SOX

EDDIE GERMANO

1988

SPRING TRAINING SKETCHBOOK
JIMMY RICE....
CRACK POW
THUMP
WHACK
JIM HAS BEEN WEARING GLASSES WHILE TAKING BATTING PRACTICE AND REALLY CRUSHING THE BALL
THE RED SOX VETERAN IS OUT TO PROVE HE'S NOT WASHED UP
F'GET IT!
WANTS TO FORGET HIS POOR '87 SEASON AND DOESN'T LIKE PEOPLE BRINGING IT UP
LINEUP
OOPS!
JIM WANTS TO PLAY EVERY DAY BUT THERE ARE THOSE WHO WANT MIKE GREENWELL IN LEFT FIELD
FRANKLY, I THINK THE SOX WILL BE WEAK IN LEFT DEFENSIVELY NO MATTER WHO PLAYS THERE AS GREENWELL HAS MUCH TO LEARN
EDDIE GERMANO, WINTER HAVEN, FLA.

SPRING TRAINING SKETCHBOOK
THE RED SOX GM, LOU GORMAN HAS A REPUTATION WITH THE KNIFE AND FORK BUT HAS EVEN A HEALTHIER APPETITE FOR BASEBALL
PASS TH' GRAVY!
THE GUY IS ALWAYS AVAILABLE FOR THE MEDIA AND LIKES TO TALK ABOUT THE CLUB
WE WON LAST NIGHT
HUH?
AN ALUMNUS OF STONEHILL COLLEGE AND PROBABLY ITS BEST PR MAN
LOU IS QUITE PLEASED WITH HIS TEAM DOWN HERE AND IS ESPECIALLY IMPRESSED WITH THE PLAYERS' ATTITUDE
EDDIE GERMANO, WINTER HAVEN, FLA.

Y'ALL WELCOME!
OWNER BEN MONDOR
PAWTUCKET
E.G.

SPRING TRAINING SKETCHBOOK
A SHOUT FOR THE SNOUT!
THE DUKE BROUGHT HIS PRESIDENTIAL CAMPAIGN TO CAMP THE PAST WEEK WHERE HE MET WITH RED SOX MANAGER JOHN McNAMARA...
BOTH MEN HAVE TWO THINGS IN COMMON... THEY WANT TO BE NO.1 AND BOTH HAVE CLASSIC PROFILES!
PHIL PHAN
EDDIE GERMANO
WINTER HAVEN, FLA

OPENING DAY BLUES
PLEASE LET'S PLAY BALL!
11 K'S WASN'T ENOUGH
EVANS' DOUBLE
HORN'S TWO-RUN SINGLE
THE FANS WERE PRAYING IT WOULDN'T RAIN
BALK
BALK
HR
THE RED SOX HAD A BIG THREE-RUN INNING IN THE 4th TO TAKE A 3-2 LEAD
WE SHUDDA GOT RAINED OUT!
ROGER CLEMENS COULD HAVE BEEN A WINNER BUT WASN'T TRULY SHARP
BALK
LATER YESTERDAY AFTERNOON... THEY WISH IT HAD
4 WALKS
34,781 FANS WERE ON HAND FOR THE OPENER
SORRY PAL, I'M HUNGRIER THAN YOU ARE!
THE NEW BOARD IN CENTER FIELD IS TRULY SOMETHING TO SEE
NOKES TIED IT AT THREE
DETROIT
3 HITS
5-3 LOSS
OWENS' ERROR HURT
YOU'RE GONNA LOVE BRADY ANDERSON
OL' PRO ALAN TRAMMELL PROVIDED THE WINNING SHOT WITH HIS TWO-RUN HOMER OFF RELIEVER LEE SMITH IN THE 10th
EDDIE GERMANO AT FENWAY PARK

A CHANGE OF HEART
THIS IS IT, I'VE HAD IT WITH THOSE 6*☆-Ѳ- RED SOX I'M GONNA PLAY GOLF
THEY ARE OUT OF THE PENNANT RACE... NO MORE BASEBALL FOR ME... I'LL GO FISHIN'!
EDDIE GERMANO

WE'LL GO CAMPING... I'M NOT GOING TO MAKE THOSE 6*☆!-Ѳ RED SOX BOTHER ME AGAIN!
YOU'VE SAID THAT BEFORE... WHAT IF THEY GO ON A LONG WIN STREAK?
GEE! DO YOU REALLY THINK THEY COULD?

STILL POSSIBLE

DESPITE ALL THEIR PROBLEMS, THE AMAZING THING IS, THE RED SOX ARE STILL ALIVE IN THE CHASE FOR 1st IN THE AMERICAN LEAGUE EAST

MANAGERIAL CHANGE RUMORS

THE BOGGS' AFFAIR

PLAYER SQUABBLES

INJURIES

ETC...

EDDIE GERMANO

HAPPY DAYS ARE HERE AGAIN

SINCE JOE MORGAN HAS TAKEN OVER THE CLUB, THE RED SOX HAVE WON FIVE STRAIGHT AND THE FANS ARE CLAMORING TO GET BACK ON THE BAND-WAGON AGAIN

RED SOX BANDWAGON

GO RED SOX

RED SOX

EDDIE GERMANO

HI-HO-HI-HO... IT'S OFF TO WORK WE GO
JOE MORGAN...
THE NEW RED SOX MANAGER IS A GREAT CHOICE... A LUNCHPAIL-TYPE OF GUY WHO HAS PAID HIS BASEBALL DUES AND WHO BELIEVES IN THE WORK ETHIC
I LIKEN JOE TO A DON CHERRY TYPE WHO CAN KICK BUTT IF THE OCCASION CALLS FOR IT
EDDIE GERMANO 7/17/88

DEAD AIM
ALL STAR BERTH
MIKE GREENWELL
HE DESERVES IT!
PHIL PHAN
EDDIE GERMANO

CRAZY WITH THE HEAT
WOW!
WHEE!
PHIL PHAN
RED SOX
POW
100
90
80
70
60
50
40
30
20
10
EDDIE GERMANO

THE STRETCH
SEPT. WINS
WE'RE HEADING FOR THE CRUCIAL MONTH OF THE SEASON KIDDIES WHEN EVERY GAME IS MIGHTY IMPORTANT
TIGERS
RED SOX
YANKEES
EDDIE GERMANO
A.L. EAST

TELLING IT LIKE IT IS
WELL, WE'RE IN FIRST PLACE BY A GAME... YOU SHOULD BE PLEASED!
REDS
PHIL PHAN
WADDAYA MEAN I SHOULD BE PLEASED... YOU SHOULD BE LEADIN' TH'EAST BY AT LEAST THREE GAMES!
REDS
AFTER THE CURRENT BALTIMORE SERIES, THE SOX PLAY 13 OF THEIR REMAINING GAMES AT HOME WHERE THE ROAD IS ALWAYS SMOOTHER
RED SOX
WHEEEE!
EDDIE GERMANO

HAUNTING MEMORIES
NY
THE GHOST OF SEASONS PAST LOOMS BIG AS THE RED SOX LOOK AHEAD TO THOSE CRUCIAL SEVEN GAMES WITH THE YANKEES AFTER THE ORIOLES
NOT THIS TIME
RED SOX
EDDIE GERMANO

WITHIN GRASP
RED SOX
1988 A.L. EASTERN DIV. PENNANT
EDDIE GERMANO

HIS ACHING TUMMY
THERE, THERE, NOW I TOLD YOU WE WOULD WIN IT!
I KNOW... BUT YOU SURE GAVE ME A BAD ATTACK OF 'AGITO!
RED SOX
1988 A.L. EAST
RED SOX
PHIL PHAN
EDDIE GERMANO

NO. ONE... WAS NO FUN
BOGGS OPENED THE GAME WITH A HIT
MOVE OVER!
BURKS ON PHILLIPS
2-1 LOSS
WHAM
BRUCE HURST DESERVED A BETTER FATE
RED SOX LEFT A MESS OF RUNNERS ON BASE
CANSECO MADE IT 1-0 FOR THE A'S

FIRE
A'S STARTER DAVE STEWART
LANSFORD DOUBLED TO LEFT...
THE ECK! STRUCK OUT BOGGS TO SAVE THE GAME FOR THE A'S
RED SOX ALUMNI ASSOC.
BOGGS HOPES FOR BETTER THINGS
...HENDERSON SINGLED TO RIGHT... AND THAT DID IT
Athletics
43
EDDIE GERMANO

WE DID IT AGAIN...LOSE!
OW!
HENDU ON BURKS...
FOR MY OL' PALS
ROGER CLEMENS THREW FIRE UNTIL THE 7th
BENZINGER BROKE UP STORM DAVIS' NO-HITTER
GIFT RUN
...THEN DROPPED RICE'S SOFT LINER
REED ON LANSFORD WAS JUST SUPER

CANSECO TIED IT UP AND...
...McGWIRE SINGLED HOME RUN NO. 3
DOIN' MY PART
BRRRR
RED SOX BATS AS COLD AS THE OCT. AIR
POW
RICH GEDMAN'S HR TIED IT UP IN THE 7th
FRIGID FENWAY
A'S WON IT IN THE 9th OFF SMITH
SOX WING IT TO OAKLAND AND THINGS LOOK DIM
EDDIE GERMANO

NOT TO WORRY
THE RED SOX ARE PLAYING IN OAKLAND TODAY AND I'M WORRIED!
WHAT ON EARTH FOR?

DO YOU REALIZE THEY HAVEN'T WON A GAME THERE ALL YEAR LONG?
GOOD! THE LAW OF AVERAGE IS ON THEIR SIDE... JUST ASK JOE MORGAN!
EDDIE GERMANO

DON'T WEEP... DESPITE THE SWEEP
4-1 LOSS
RED SOX
A'S
3 HRS IN SERIES
OAKLAND A'S 1988 A.L. CHAMPS
THE RED SOX APPEARED LETHARGIC
JOSE CANSECO IS AMONG THE TOP PLAYERS IN THE GAME
LET'S TAKE SOLACE FANS... THE A'S WERE THE BETTER TEAM
THE ECK IS SOMETHING
DAVE STEWART PROVED HE CAN REALLY PITCH

THE SOX HEAD FOR HOME...
...AND THE A'S HEAD FOR THE WORLD SERIES
FINALLY A TIP OF THE HAT TO SKIPPER JOE MORGAN... HE MADE A DRAB SEASON EXCITING
PLAY IT AGAIN, JOE
PHIL PHAN
EDDIE GERMANO

A CLOSED BOOK
BOSTON RED SOX
1988 AMERICAN LEAGUE
EASTERN DIVISION
CHAMPIONS
1988
BOSTON
RED SOX
LOSING FOUR STRAIGHT TO A GREAT TEAM LIKE TH' A'S IS NO DISGRACE... ALL WE HAVE TO DO IS PLUG A FEW HOLES FOR NEXT YEAR!
PHIL PHAN
© EDDIE GERMANO

IT'S OUT OF SIGHT!
PLAY BALL!
RED SOX
FORGET YOUR PROBLEMS KIDDIES... IT'S BASEBALL TIME AGAIN!
B
PHIL PHAN
EDDIE GERMANO